DEADLY PAST

Welcome to Lake Pines.
A fictional small town in Northwestern Ontario that is home to both year-round residents and summer cottagers. Hidden secrets, private lives, and tension lay the groundwork for treacherous crimes. But there are more than secrets buried in this small town.

Order of Books in this series:

LAKE PINES MURDER MYSTERY SERIES

Murder At First Light
Death At Deception Bay
Murder Of Crows
The Dead Of Winter
The Night Is Darkest
Conspiracy of Blood
Deadly Past
Echoes of Guilt

DEADLY PAST

A gripping Lake Pines Mystery

Cover designed by Warren Design

L.L. Abbott
www.LLAbbott.com

Paperback ISBN 978-1-989325-71-1
Large Print ISBN 978-1-989325-73-5

This story is for Kate, always a true friend
and a great cheerleader.
Thank you for sharing your island, and the propellor that sparked a tale.
And for Drew, for always being there.

DEADLY PAST

*"As bad as things were,
the worst was yet to come."*

1

Ten Years Earlier. Lake Pines, Ontario.

Wayne Burgess looked at the newspaper in his hands and nervously crumpled it in his grip. He had tumbled out of bed that morning, reluctantly and full of agitation, unable to sleep since it happened.

The cold, damp surroundings tightened around his chest, his stomach twisting each time he looked out the window. He had always loved this small one-level cabin nestled in the middle of the field, located on the outskirts of town. Until recently, he had never thought too much about the simple construction, with its peaked roof that mounted in the middle and two small rooms that extended off each side of the building. The cabin had been in his family since his great grandfather built it generations earlier, and it was always a place of peaceful family tranquility.

The small stone fireplace encouraged stories and where, as a family, they'd gather for the Christmas holidays. Simple traditions were created hanging their stockings and debating over which side of the fireplace they should place the tree, and they remained some of Wayne's fondest memories. The cabin was far away from the noise of Lake Pines, with only the wind and snow to fill the imaginations of two small boys.

Josh had moved to Toronto a year earlier, and Wayne was thankful that his brother left before he could learn what happened at their childhood retreat. It was the cabin where he and his younger brother fought for dominance on the Scrabble board, and where the two found adventure and solace in both their extensive Hardy Boys collection and the surrounding forest. The curved hills drew the two boys outside with the lure of tobogganing thrills and battle reenactments and as they grew older, they would sit and talk as the sun fell below the horizon.

Now those same curved hills, left undisturbed by toboggan rides long forgotten, flowed freely with tall prairie grass. Except for one patch of ground where a fresh mound of dirt disfigured the land, the property looked abandoned.

No longer was the cabin a place of solace, but because of what happened, it had become a place of secrets.

Then he saw something in the distance, or rather someone. It was Carly Phillips, his best friend's younger sister, and the person who was at the center of the event that changed everything in their lives.

Carly was a sweet girl. She was adventurous, as long as the adventure never took her too far away from Lake Pines. Her fiery red hair, with sweeping curls and unruly green eyes, attracted the attention of most kids in their school. Often it was the fear of her older brother Simon that prompted those glares to go no further.

Wayne swallowed down his nervousness, knowing that the worst of what they had done was behind them. He caught his reflection in the windowpane and wondered how he found himself in such a difficult position. He was an athletic and friendly teen and didn't need anyone to tell him that, nor did he need the provincial trophy that rested on his shelf to prove it. He was proud and confident of who he was. He also knew that, beyond all else, he was a loyal friend.

His friends believed he would become a doctor, or a healer of some sort, after he had brought an injured blackbird back from the brink of death after it flew at full force into the side of a window. He cradled the bird, rested it in a box of shredded paper, and fed it drops of sugar water until it recuperated enough to flap its wings and soar out of the box.

Instead, Wayne dreamed of becoming a cop and he followed Constable Peter George as he patrolled Main Street, peppering the young, personable officer with questions about what qualifications he needed to join the Lake Pines police force. The senior police officer, amused by the eager teen, soon took him under his wing and taught him the daily routines and expectations of the job.

As Wayne stood waiting in the empty cabin, he dropped his eyes to the paper in his hands and let out a heaving sigh. As he did, he closed his eyes and prayed that he was dreaming. That there would be some slight change in his surroundings. But when he opened his eyes, the hill and the mound of dirt were still there.

The drizzling rain tapped against the window and Wayne's pulse quickened with each step that Carly took, bringing her closer to the cabin. As Wayne stepped outside and Carly came closer, he could see the tears in her eyes. There was also a shadow behind her that Wayne hadn't noticed earlier, and he held his breath as the man walked around Carly, past Wayne, and into the cabin.

They had arrived because they needed to deal with what happened. The terror had forced them into the decision they made two days earlier, and they needed a plan.

Carly's father was just shy of six feet, and his broad shoulders and firm, wide hands were the gifts of hard labor and genetics.

"Have you mentioned anything to anyone?" Mr. Phillips asked as he looked out the window, into the field, and over the hill beyond the cabin.

Wayne shook his head. He looked over his shoulder and out the window, following Mr. Phillips' gaze.

Wayne, even more nervous, still gripped the newspaper as he replied, "They're looking for him!"

They glanced at each other, no one wanting to be the next to speak.

"What happened was not your fault," Mr. Phillips rested a hand on Wayne's shoulder. "And there's no reason to ruin both of your lives over this." He then looked at his daughter, who was hugging her tiny frame with shaking arms. "You saved Carly, and I'll never forget that Wayne."

"What about Simon?" The one person Wayne never kept a secret from was the one person they all knew they shouldn't tell.

Wayne had opted out of the fishing retreat that kept Simon out of Lake Pines for the last five days when

Constable Peter George invited him to work at the town fair as a cadet, and he jumped at the opportunity.

It was the reason that Wayne was walking along the edge of the city park when Carly was trying to flee. And it was Wayne who was holding Carly when the last push sent John Turshen over the side of the bluff. Although it was her desperate measure to be free of the man who was trying to hurt her, it was still a push that killed the mayor's son and would have both Carly and Wayne in front of a judge and charged with his murder by the end of the week.

Protection shrouded John Turshen because of his father's position in the small town, and although the wave of nepotism was waning, it had been in place long enough that the girls that leveled complaints against John's aggressive actions found they were being treated as criminals instead of victims. John frequently bullied other kids, and his father continuously mended transgressions with teachers, leaving his reputation intact. Even though everyone in town knew what John was capable of, it would be near impossible to prove in court.

"I think it's best we don't tell him," Mr. Phillips said, making it the last thing they said about the matter.

The rain pounded down harder, blurring the view of the hill beyond the cabin. The grave that the three of them dug on the night John fell to his death would hide in the grass that would eventually regrow over the loose earth, and the body of the person who attacked many girls would remain hidden.

It would be a deadly past that could come back to haunt them. But the only people who knew the truth about what happened were standing inside the small, damp cabin looking out at the hill, and they each vowed that their secret would forever remain hidden.

2

36 hours earlier. Warroad, Minnesota

He waited next to the chainlink fence, hidden from the glare of the overhanging light, trying to keep from falling down.

The drive northeast from Grand Forks was shorter than he thought it would be but was more difficult than it should have been because of the northerly gusts that pushed across the highway. For the last thirteen months, he had been deeply ensconced in the same organization which was strategically organizing to shut down the vaccination production facility in Ohio. But it was his work over the last seven months that had put his life in danger and now had him hiding next to the metal fence that surrounded the small airport at the southwest tip of Lake of the Woods. He was alone and holding the documented proof that would bring down Dennis Nathanson while he waited for his contact to arrive.

Alone is how he had been since his wife of fifteen years fell sick leaving him with a young son and guilt over the part he played in her contracting the virus that cut her life short. His disbelief in the virus and the true impact it was having on the world, left him open to persuasion when a junior staffer from Dennis Nathanson's office approached him.

They were going to make things stronger and more reliable by controlling the spread of propaganda, but in reality, it was Nathanson's office that had done the worst damage.

He looked into the dark field and over the water just beyond where he was supposed to meet his contact. The night was silent, except for the rustling wind combing the trees in the nearby forest. More worrisome, however, was the absence of the approaching plane he was waiting for. He pulled the zipper of his windbreaker up, sealing his jacket close to his neck, and patted the inside pocket of his jacket. He felt the crumple of the envelope and relaxed his shoulders. It would be less than an hour to fly to the island, just south of Sioux Narrows and once he was there, he'd put an end to what Nathanson and the group in his office had done.

Until then, he just hoped he wouldn't be seen. If anyone had stumbled across him as he waited in the shadows of the vacant lot, they would have assumed he was a junkie. Cold sweat coated his skin, and he struggled to hold his head straight or speak without slurs. A border guard would have pulled him aside, no matter what his government identification read. Travel restrictions that had been put in place during the global pandemic had made airports and land borders even tougher to cross, especially to anyone who seemed unwell.

Fever. Labored breathing. Sweaty brows. All became the warning signs of danger that had temporarily superseded the search for scissors, lighters, and large bottles of water. And his permission to carry a weapon had never caused him any issues at the border, but today he left his gun in the glovebox of his car, just in the event he was stopped and questioned.

He wasn't armed, and usually, he never needed to be. His expert training and peak physical condition had seen him work his way out of several awkward situations while he was on covert missions. There was never a break in his training and exercise routine, even when he had been reassigned to the senator's office. Daily runs and a nutritionally sound diet had never taken a break, even when his operations changed from infiltrating foreign governments to sabotaging domestic businesses. But all of his training and good health couldn't fight what was happening now. He shivered, not because of the chill in the air but because of the toxin that was taking hold inside his body.

He glanced at the time, his contact was ten minutes late. He stepped forward, out of the shadow, and was near his car when he heard the familiar hum in the distance. The light in the sky wobbled and the Cessna fought against the wind as the pilot dropped closer to the surface of the water. He reached into his pocket and pulled out the small plastic bottle and shook out two small white pills and swallowed them dry, and after a few seconds, he tipped out one more. The flight would be difficult if he was fighting back the pain and he needed to make sure he reached the island before it was too late.

Forcing the movement in his legs, he jogged toward the shoreline. The manicured lawn that stretched out next to the water would be filled with families enjoying the final days of summer hours after sunrise. Even with the cooler temperatures, the die-hard water lovers found a way to enjoy the final days of the season before the first snow flakes fell and a thin surface of ice began to form. Now, however, it was lit only with the soft glow cast from the light in the parking lot behind him.

Flying floatplanes at night was illegal, and he had used all the favors he accumulated with his contact to have the plane delivered at this remote dock. After all, he knew he'd never live long enough to collect after tonight. His steps slowed when he reached the dock and his head swirled as he stepped onto the floating structure. He paced each step as he made his way to the end of the dock just as the plane came to a full stop.

His contact climbed out and walked past him without any comments or conversation, and the agent climbed up and closed the door. It had been many years since he flew a float plane and each move and motion came back to him instinctively. Like walking, flying float planes was a way of life in his youth and it occurred to him that it was ironic that this may be his final flight.

The forty-minute trip, mired only by a strong wind and dark sky, gave him time to consider the last year of his life. Had he done all he could for his son? He knew he failed his wife, but leaving his son with his grandparents and no note was the only way he could ensure his safety. He just wished there was a better way.

It was almost one o'clock in the morning and the open water stretched out below. The shoreline, curved and shaped by glaciers left more than ten thousand islands that dotted Lake of the Woods. Dark blue shadows cast across the water's surface marking islands and inlets. As he flew closer to his destination he dropped his altitude and followed along the same path he did when he first received his pilot's license and worked for one of the fishing camps in Whitefish Bay.

His love of flying guided him toward his work with the fishing camps, and it was during one of the many trips that he was introduced to the eager politician who would become the senator he was now trying to stop. Now it was this same path he was flying along that would, hopefully, correct all he had done wrong since he worked with that same man.

Landing in the Aulneau Peninsula was one of his preferred locations to set down a plane. Finding the correct pitch, and angling the rudders was the equivalent to conducting an orchestra. Working in conjunction with the wind, temperature, and then ultimately the current - brought together thousands of hours of experience to create the perfect landing. And each time he would arrive with a new visitor to the area he'd see the reflection of wonder in their eyes. The awes and oohs that passengers moaned as he drifted toward the dock, their faces pushed against the small aircraft's windows as they stared in disbelief that such a smooth landing could be made in the wilderness. It was a point of pride.

As he recalled those moments, he flew his plane closer to the water. The wind had subsided and the clouds had cleared in spots, revealing streams of moonlight over the water's surface. The calmness of the water and the stillness of the night briefly cleared his mind and he glided into a perfect landing, drifting with the current and toward the small island.

His destination was to the small private island, owned by the man who was funding their entire operation. His connections within both Canada and the U.S. allowed him to establish a permanent blur on satellite or internet-mapped images, meaning the Cessna's approach and arrival to the island would also be hidden.

As the plane neared the island, he closed the throttle, cut the engine, and let the current pull him the final stretch toward the dock. The lapping sounds of the water against the hull on the floats and against the rocky shore were like a call welcoming him home and he let out a deep sigh of relief as he stepped out of the plane and onto the dock.

The cabin was dark and he knew that even though he failed to reach the lead agent, that he would have received the message that he was coming. His stomach twisted in pain, the pills had worn off during the flight and were failing to suppress the sting of the toxin that was slowly killing him.

He climbed the steep hill at the end of the dock, and he struggled with each step he took. Fallen branches and dried leaves were piled on a patch of rock waiting to be lit for a bonfire, and a faint hum of the pumphouse drifted down from behind the cabin. Other than that, there was no noise.

There was no warning. No stabbing pain. No violent attack. When he collapsed at the top of the hill, his body surrendered to the toxin, and his limbs were paralyzed. The pills he took less than an hour earlier, dulled his senses to the approaching pain and shielded him from any warning. His heart was weakening and he could no longer find the energy to gasp for air or scream out for help. He fell to his knees and then forward on his hands.

Dry pine needles pierced his palms and loose rocks pressed against his flesh. Every tissue on the surface of his skin violently reacted to the slight breeze or the temperature change. His body was shutting down, and although he didn't know how long he had, he knew it wasn't long.

His face pressed against the cold rock and he turned toward the water, and eventually, his entire body dropped. He landed with his arms folded under his torso, but even if they hadn't been compressed by his fall, he wouldn't have had the strength to reach out. He was completely still. Paralyzed by the toxin. But his eyes remained focused on the boot that stopped beside him. They were black, scuffed, and marked with dried mud.

He recognized them and knew who they belonged to. He knew who was wearing them and what the man had come for. What he didn't know was how long he had been standing there. His breath was growing weak, and his heartbeat was ragged.

The man turned his fallen friend over, unzipped his coat, and slipped his hand inside. He slid the envelope out of the pocket and focused on the man's eyes as he lay motionless, unable to fight back.

The agent watched as his friend walked away, holding the envelope and the proof he had fought so hard to obtain.

The clouds cast a shadow across the island and the faint glow of the orange sunrise tinted the rock near the water. His body stopped shaking as his chest tightened with each painful, labored breath. He had failed. And as he lay dying it was the image of his wife and son that remained with him as he took his final breath.

3

Present Day.

Despite the glare of the setting sun that crept through the small crack in the roof and streaked across the dirt-covered planks, the chill from the near-frozen ground was making its way into the space where Chloe huddled. A tremor crawled through her body each time she considered her situation.

Her eyes darted toward the shadow on the floor, as a cockroach scurried across the bottom of her mattress before it made its way through the space in the wall, disappearing into the grain storage bins. On the first night she arrived, the sight of the pests caused her to scream. Much to the delight of the men who watched her every move, and they both laughed as she jumped back, trying to avoid being near it. Chloe learned to fear the men more than the roaches, but less than the rats, who also seemed to find their way next to her in the middle of the night.

Enough weeks had gone by that she knew they had kept her locked up for several months, but not quite the length of two seasons. She saw some people leave and others arrive. However, never on their own accord, and as of a week ago, only five remained.

She didn't know where they came from or where they were going. No one asked because everyone was afraid of the answer. Apart from a few girls, Chloe spoke to no one. She didn't want to draw any unwanted attention. Instead, she focused on an opportunity to escape and after a long while, it finally presented itself.

She attempted to break free once before, and the painful echoes of the cries for help tugged at her conscience. Others, just like her, wanted to escape and be free from their nightmare, and her instinct was to turn back. However, it was her slight hesitation that gave her captors just enough time to reach her.

Within minutes, Chloe was back where she began, along with the others who were being held in individual units. Latched in like prisoners and sedated every evening, there were few opportunities to break free. Chloe was one of the last people to be brought to the holding cells, and she still had some energy left to fight and some hope of escape. Within the first few nights of being abducted, Chloe realized that much of both were lost to the other captives.

But it was when Chloe looked into the blank eyes of the young teen in the cell next to her she vowed to not give up fighting for her freedom. With what little strength she had left, she plotted her escape once again.

Although she had lost track of the number of weeks, she knew it had only been two days since the last time she tried to break free. It was guilt that caused her to turn back the first time, but now she couldn't risk missing the last opportunity she had for freedom, and she would block out the voices of the other prisoners and focus on her escape.

No matter what the cost.

Although her plan was simple, she knew it would take a miracle to pull off, and she patiently waited for the right moment.

A yellow-tinged light from the far end of the room flooded the dark space as the shortest of the two men kicked it open. Chloe breathed a sigh of relief. Although she never would have described either of the two men as 'good people', he was the least offensive.

He was thick, however, he wasn't fat or strong. He walked with a casual gait, and he wore his sandy brown hair in a shoulder-length feathered cut, one that most boys rarely attempted but it seemed to work for his round face. Chloe thought he could be mistaken as a friendly member of a choir group instead of the mastermind that had been responsible for her abduction.

The rattling of the small bowls on the metal tray echoed in time with each of his shuffling steps as he made his way and then stopped at each unit.

Units were what Chloe preferred to call them. As opposed to cages, which is what they were, separated only by thin sheets that hung from the metal bars. Rudimentary in their structure, built for containment and housed in a fifty-year-old barn that sat in the center of a derelict farm. It was a place where no one would question the coming and going of their truck in the middle of the night, and far enough away from anyone who could hear the screams of the captives inside.

Initially, Chloe shared her space with three other girls, but over the last week, people were being transported away and they kept the five remaining souls separated.

Chloe counted under her breath. She was at the furthest end of the row of units, counting each of his steps as she lay motionless, facing away from view. She steadied her breathing and focused on the plan she had worked out over the last twenty-four hours. Everything needed to look natural and unplanned if this was going to work. She was too weak to fight either of the men holding her in the barn, so she needed to work around that if she was going to escape. And ever since her first escape attempt, extra care was taken to keep her under tight watch.

"Supper," he announced as he slipped his key into the lock and then swung the gate open. "It's your favorite."

The mocking tone didn't rile Chloe the way it did the first few weeks, instead it deepened her resolve to escape. As he bent over to place the tray on the floor, Chloe stood from where she lay on the mattress and stumbled on her first step, falling forward and onto the tray.

"Damn it!" he yelled as he tried to avoid being knocked to the ground.

Chloe fell to the floor and scrambled to her feet when the guard nudged her with his foot, holding a piece of bread hidden in her clutches. As he stooped to pick up the tray, muttering obscenities under his breath, Chloe pushed her back against the bars of the cell and grabbed the padlock. The distraction worked better than she had hoped and gave her just enough time to push the squished piece of bread into the lock.

He picked up the bowl, still half full of the watered-down broth, and placed it on the floor next to Chloe's mattress, and tossed the bottle of water beside it.

"Make it last. That's all you're getting until morning," he snapped. Then he pulled the familiar blue and white pills out of his pocket and watched as Chloe placed them on her tongue. He squeezed the bottom of her jaw, forcing her mouth open, and poked his finger along her cheek to make sure she swallowed.

He pushed past Chloe and pulled the gate closed and slipped the padlock back through the latch. As the guard cursed her clumsiness, he focused on wiping the stain of the soup from his pants and didn't notice the absence of the clicking sound as he pushed the lock closed.

"Lights out and don't make a sound!"

They were the last seven words Chloe heard every evening just before she lost consciousness, and she swore that this would be the last time.

She waited until the sounds of his footsteps faded to a shuffle and then disappeared completely before she tugged the padlock and twisted the shackle out from between the bars.

They kept the outer door of the building unlocked until after their last inspection of the night, and she counted on their strict routine and lack of deviation from their schedule as she dashed through the empty building. Chloe clenched her teeth and tightened her diaphragm, making as little noise as she could. She ran through the darkened room and tried to silence each step and breath in the cavernous space.

Heavy black chains hung from the roof beams and a long row of tall metal jugs, rusted and dented with wear, lined the wall next to the exit.

She thrust her body against the thick wooden door and struggled against the weight, which was now exacerbated by the heavy haze clouding her conscience and was robbing her of a clear focus.

An unrelenting wind rattled the side of the old barn, knocking the hardened and weathered planks against the heavy beams, masking the sound of the hinge as it squealed against the rust that coated the metal.

A cast-iron latch bar was all that stood between Chloe and her freedom. The oversized door, which reached over ten feet high, hung crookedly and wedged tightly into its frame with corroded metal hinges. The last fifty years had also shifted the oversized panel, causing it to drag into the hardened ground with each opening. Each sound the metal bar made, echoed in the surrounding space. She couldn't be sure if the sound of the door scraping across the ground or the howling of the wind seeping through the slight opening would reach the farthest end of the building, but one thing she knew was that she needed to work quickly. Each squeak of the iron handle, or scrape of the wooden door, threatened to reveal her escape.

The effects of the sedative were taking hold, blurring her vision, and slowing her movements. Her hands and mind moved at different speeds and made the work of wiggling the bar loose and opening the door difficult.

Finally, after several attempts, she lifted the bar from the latch and pushed the door open. Chloe squeezed her lids shut and shook her head before forcing her eyes wide and peering out into the night, praying that she'd remain unnoticed as she forced her body through the opening.

And then she ran.

This time refusing to look back - for fear that she wouldn't have the strength to continue to run.

Her bare feet felt the sting of the cold that settled into the ground at nightfall and jolted her entire body awake. With only a slight glint of light on the horizon, Chloe broke into as fast of a run as she could manage, crossing the vast field with only her willpower to guide her. Unaware of where she was going, or if she was even heading in the right direction.

Each step brought an uncertain landing on either an uneven surface or a sharp rock. Biting her lip was the only thing she could do to stifle the scream that was rising in her throat each time a twig or stone pierced the bottoms of her feet. She didn't care if she wouldn't be able to walk after tonight if it just meant being free.

The steely gray of the storm clouds threatened rain, but tonight, they also protected her from being seen by the full moon that was nestled behind them. Silver-fringed clouds pushed over the hills and cast a dark shadow over the barn. The faded wooden exterior perfectly concealed the steel walls and padlocked cells inside. To any passerby, it looked like a neglected farm along the side of a rural road. But for Chloe and the few remaining survivors, it concealed the worst nightmare imaginable.

The bitter, chalky taste of the pills was clogging her throat, and Chloe could feel her legs weaken under its increasing effects. She knew from experience that she had less than half an hour before disorientation would engulf her. Until then, she had to focus on reaching the road.

Chloe's pace slowed and she could tell by the pull in her muscles and the angle of her body that she reached a hill. Her breathing became heavier and each muscle in her leg was fighting her steps as she made her way to the top. Chloe's foot landed in a shallow hole, twisting her ankle and buckling her leg at her knee. The painful heat seared up her calf and through her thigh, setting her escape back several paces as her body spiraled backward, landing her at the bottom of the hill.

She scrambled to her feet and hobbled the final distance until she reached the gate. The swelling around her ankle brought a searing heat to her skin and a stabbing pain with each move. She tugged the rope and pulled the latch loose and hobbled through the gate, letting it fall closed behind her.

Free from the shadow of the trees, Chloe could see a faint haze of light in the distance. She had reached the road and could hear the distant hum of traffic over the hill. The cold pavement brought a tingling relief to the bottom of her feet and she stumbled against the pain as she made her way toward the light.

Her head swayed as her neck wobbled and she focused on the memory of her mother as she pushed against the effects of the pills that were fighting to pull her under. It was the argument and the last words they yelled at each other that Chloe replayed in her mind. Over the hours and days and weeks that she was being held, she thought of little else.

How trivial their fight seemed now, and she longed for the overprotectiveness that she was so eager to shun.

A bright yellow light pulled her away from her thoughts as it stretched across the top of the pavement where the road curved over the hill. Growing in intensity and height as the truck mounted the peak.

Chloe stumbled across the pavement and lifted her arms over her head, hoping the driver would recognize her signal for help. The horn blared as the lights came closer, but Chloe refused to move.

Death would be preferable to being back where she started less than a half-hour ago. The truck driver would save her - one way or another.

As she fell to her knees, the brakes screeched, the sound rebounding off the dense forest that lined the opposite side of the road. It would only be a matter of time before she was free from the hell she had been living. Chloe closed her eyes, no longer having the strength to either scream or cry, and collapsed on the ground.

Sounds grew hollow and more distant as she faded into unconsciousness, but it was the sour scent of coffee and heavy fuel that pulled Chloe's eyes open.

She was staring into the panicked eyes of the driver, who was shaking her awake, and he didn't stop until Chloe pushed her body sideways and was sick across the pavement. This, the driver quickly assessed, was not a stranded hitchhiker. He lifted Chloe and cradled her thin, shaking body in his arms.

His rough, burly hands and smoke-filled clothes overwhelmed her as he lifted her into the cab of his truck and closed the door.

Every action lingered, as if Chloe was watching a scene play out on a broken movie projector. She and the driver, each playing the roles of two miscast characters in a horror film. Chloe opened her mouth to speak, but she was unable to make the sound that her lips were forming. She could feel her body being moved into the cab of the truck, and the door being closed beside her body, and then her head tumbling uncontrollably into the back of the headrest. A pine air freshener waved under the rear-view mirror and her arms pushed against a discarded paper bag that held the half-eaten remains of a burger. And again, she felt like she was going to be sick.

The driver climbed into the cab, slammed the door shut, and mumbled something about being lost and getting to a hospital as Chloe's eyes closed.

For the first time since she had been abducted, she felt like she could stop fighting.

The engine rumbled, and the truck lurched forward as the driver shifted into gear. Chloe tilted her head and gazed out the window and across the field that she had just run through. The clouds had cleared, and the slim silvery lining had transformed into a bright beam that illuminated the barn and the path she ran.

Chloe's breathing became steady as the truck moved away from the barn and the nightmare she had been living. The driver peppered Chloe with questions, but she didn't have the energy to answer, and tears without the sound of sobs rolled down her face. He eventually fell silent as he steered his truck toward the highway and headed directly to the hospital.

He radioed ahead, alerting the police to the injured passenger he was transporting. Chloe tried to understand his words, many distorted due to her failing senses, but the one thing she heard clearly was his name. Gary.

Gary was bringing her to safety, but she knew it would be nothing like freedom. Especially with what still lay ahead and what remained behind.

4

Kerry pulled her arms through her coat and tucked her gloves into her pocket before picking Dominique up from her playmat. She nuzzled her nose into the crux of her daughter's neck and took a deep breath. She never tired of Dominique's fresh baby scent, and she always made sure it was the last thing she did before she left for work.

Dominique giggled as Kerry plastered her with kisses.

"We'll stop by your office this afternoon when we're out for our walk," Oliver reached out and tucked his hands gently under his granddaughter's arms and pulled her into the air. "Wave bye-bye to mommy."

Oliver grabbed Dominique's hand and shook it in the air and then snuggled the small child under his chin. Oliver arrived on the same day Kerry and Simon adopted Dominique, and after a brief visit, returned to Montreal just as the warnings for the global pandemic were sweeping across the country.

Kerry rushed to Montreal to help pack her father's things and move him to Lake Pines for the duration of the lockdown. The world was afraid. Stories of the black plague and international espionage populated the internet and news. It was difficult to know how to make sense of the virus. Even with Kerry's many connections in the medical field, everything was so new, and no one could predict what would happen. But one thing was certain. People were dying.

They had missed the opportunity to return to Lake Pines before the government put travel restrictions in place, forcing Kerry to remain in Montreal for almost three weeks. Until they could travel west, Kerry wanted to feel useful in the face of an unprecedented health crisis and volunteered at the hospital.

The emergency room brought horrors that Kerry learned weren't exaggerated versions of the virus, but the actual virus itself. Doctors had come out of retirement to fill the spaces needed in emergency rooms and makeshift medical facilities, and Kerry did what she could to help the nurses and doctors on the frontline. The rise of groups trying to block the production of the vaccine with their misplaced ideas and theories exacerbated the stress being felt in the hospitals.

Calls home were Kerry's only connection to Simon and Dominique and she was growing frightened that she may never see them again. Then, upon Oliver's suggestion, they packed up the car and drove through two days and two nights until they reached Lake Pines.

Once they were safely home and had isolated themselves for two weeks in the basement, both Kerry and Simon decided it would be best if Oliver remained in Lake Pines, even if it was only until the threat of the pandemic passed.

That was more than a year ago, and Oliver decided to settle in Lake Pines. He was eager to continue to spend his days watching his granddaughter grow and explore the world around her.

Dominique had grown so close to her grandfather that Kerry and Simon knew it would be unfair to separate them. Even though vaccination rates were high and the worst of the health threats had seemed to pass, both Kerry and Simon thought it would be best to continue with the current arrangement of Oliver helping to care for Dominique at their home.

And that's exactly what they did, Simon further insisting that he convert the space above the garage into a private apartment where Oliver could live. Still keeping his independence while he remained close.

"Oh, and by the way, Wayne is coming into town for a few weeks and he said he's going to finish installing that small woodstove Simon picked up a month ago,"

Kerry wrapped her scarf around her neck before tucking the end into the top of her jacket.

"It'll be good to see him again," Oliver said. "I'll pick up some of that beer he likes when I'm out today."

Dominique wiggled in Oliver's arms and he lowered her to the playmat and she crawled over to the stuffed bear that Raven was resting his chin on.

"Thanks," Kerry kissed her father on the cheek. "I may be a little later tonight because I'm going to see Gloria later."

Oliver pressed his lips together and tilted his head at the mention of the adoption counselor's name.

Kerry raised her hand before he said anything, "I know what you think, but I made my mind up."

"And what does Simon think?"

The look on Kerry's face answered Oliver's question.

"You didn't tell him what you're planning on doing, did you?"

Kerry shook her head.

"Be careful, Kerry," Oliver warned. "You might not be prepared for the information Gloria has."

Kerry hugged her father and Dominique once more before finally leaving the house, ignoring her father's comment.

Kerry tried her best to forget the worries and restrictions that altered their lives during the pandemic, but each trip to a store or restaurant brought back the familiar fears, and she found she was avoiding friends because of it. Over the last month, she had made a concerted effort to return to her normal daily routines. Before the pandemic, her morning routine always included a stop at Lisa's café. The restrictions forced many changes in people's lives and habits had changed and routines altered.

Almost overnight, towns and cities seemed abandoned. First, by those abiding by the shelter in place orders, followed by the forced closure of restaurants and shops. Main Street was disfigured. Even when restrictions relaxed, most businesses realized they couldn't afford to remain open. The river of debt that flowed through the town's businesses wiped away essential services and part of the area's culture and charm.

Eventually, some businesses reopened and their customers returned. Nods and waves eventually shifted to shouts of 'hello' and hugs. But not immediately. People were leery of returning to their lives after spending so many months afraid of something they couldn't see. Trust would be difficult without proof of their safety. But people learned how to trust and relax and they returned to their lives, everyone eager to fall back into a normal pattern.

Those on the front line celebrated the final vestige of excitement last, reserving their joy after having experienced several false alarms. But this was real. The vaccine had worked.

It was the day Kerry watched Lisa unlock her café doors, tears flowing from her eyes and those of her patrons, that she felt relief. Customers congregated at tables, forming their familiar group of friends together. All feeling rebellious without masks and vowing to never take their freedom and health for granted.

Kerry continued her routine of stopping at Lisa's café and would add extra time to greet neighbors and have a few conversations. She, too, realized the importance of not taking these moments for granted and pushed her fear aside.

Her morning passed quickly and after lunch, her visit with Dominique helped carry her through until the late afternoon when she turned off the lights, locked the door, and drove directly to Gloria's office.

When Kerry had called to make an appointment at the adoption agency, Gloria believed it was because she and Simon were looking to adopt a second child. In fact, it was because of Dominique that Kerry was eager to speak with the counselor.

Gloria was waiting for Kerry when she arrived and they spent the first ten minutes gushing over the latest photos that Kerry had taken of Dominique and had stored on her phone.

Kerry paused on a picture that Oliver took during Dominique's birthday celebration.

"Is your dad still here?" Gloria asked as she sat down in a chair and Kerry followed and sat in the one next to her.

"Yeah, he's been amazing," Kerry said. "And with all the concerns during the pandemic lockdown, he ended up being the perfect childcare option for us."

"You're very blessed, Kerry," Gloria rested her hand on Kerry's arm and smiled. Gloria remained one of the most colorful individuals that Kerry knew. Her bright blue framed glasses replaced the cherry red ones that Gloria wore on the first day Kerry met her, and she painted her nails to match. Silver streaks naturally highlighted her midnight black hair, not adding years to her face but illuminating her personality. But one thing remained the same, Gloria's warm and caring disposition for the children and families she brought together.

"I'm so excited that you and Simon are looking to expand your family," Gloria gushed as she folded her hands together and tucked them under her chin.

"That's not why I wanted to see you," Kerry confessed. "Although, it *is* about Dominique."

The ends of Gloria's smile sagged, and concern flooded her face. "Is everything okay?"

Kerry nodded, "Yes, but ever since her first birthday I have been thinking of her birth mother."

Gloria lowered her hands into her lap and pressed her lips together into a sympathetic smile and listened while Kerry spoke.

"I don't want Dominique to feel that we took her from a life that she should've had."

"Dominique is very lucky to have found you and Simon. I hope you believe that."

"We do. There isn't a day that goes by that either of us feels anything but grateful, but,..." Kerry's words hung in the air between them.

"But," Gloria continued, "you want to make sure."

Kerry let out a deep sigh. "Exactly."

"There's probably not much I can tell you. It really depends on what the birth parents had agreed to. Although there are open adoptions, some mothers want their names and situations kept private for various reasons."

"Could you at least check?" Kerry begged.

Gloria waited for a few seconds and then stood and walked to her desk. She tapped her fingers across the keyboard and wiggled her mouse and clicked several links until her eyes settled on a file.

After a few awkward seconds, Kerry asked, "Did you find something?

"Not much," Gloria spoke but left her eyes transfixed on her computer screen. "Dominique's birth mom arrived at the hospital in an ambulance about an hour before she gave birth."

"Was the father with her?"

"There doesn't appear to be any record of the father on file."

"Had she always planned on adoption for her baby?"

"The hospital records show it was the first time that she had ever been at that hospital. She wasn't registered with a doctor in Lake Pines."

Gloria rested her chin on her right hand and continued to read, "A passerby found her lying on the road and they called the ambulance. Apparently, she had been the victim of a hit and run."

Kerry couldn't control the tears that came to her eyes and then rolled down her cheeks. Even though she didn't know Dominique's birth mother, she felt connected to her and felt the sting of sadness when she thought of her in pain.

"What happened?"

"Just before she went into labor, she insisted on speaking with a nurse about putting her baby up for adoption," Gloria turned her eyes from the screen to

Kerry's face. "She signed the papers just before she fell unconscious. Dominique was born via an emergency c-section."

"And her birth mom? What happened? Did she recover alright?" Kerry was sitting on the edge of her seat, waiting for Gloria's answer.

"I'm sorry, Kerry, but she died. She had lost too much blood by the time they brought her to the hospital emergency room."

Kerry folded her hands over her mouth and cried. Gloria rushed around her desk and wrapped her arms around Kerry's shoulders and held her until she wiped the last of the tears from her cheeks.

"Was the driver who hit her ever caught?"

Gloria shook her head.

"Can you tell me her name?"

Gloria paused and then said, "Katie Lancaster."

5

Chloe rolled over, pushing her face into the pillow, as the door opened and a flood of noise from the hallway seeped in, crushing the surrounding silence. Two days had passed since Chloe arrived in the emergency room at Lake Pines Hospital after Gary found her in the middle of the road and it was two long days since she had escaped. That time had also passed without Chloe speaking a single word to any of the doctors or nurses.

Doctor Scotswood had returned, followed by Julie, the cherubic nurse who first treated Chloe. They made their way across the oversized hospital room, normally outfitted with four beds, but reserved as a private room for Chloe's recovery.

She learned to recognize the tap-tap-tap of Doctor Scotswood's straight, measured gait and the shush-shush-shush of Julie's rubber sandals as they walked toward her bed. It was an unfortunate skill she gained during her time in captivity, one that she used as a way of deciphering between the two men who concealed her, along with others, in the barn.

Survival mechanisms, the first trauma therapist had explained, would have inserted themselves naturally during the months of her captivity. She warned Chloe they could reappear at any moment without warning.

Chloe had always been sensitive to sounds and smells when she was a child. Her mother always claimed it was because of the energetic music and rustic cooking she provided. However, that had changed. Now, Chloe had to force her attention to recognize even the weak aroma of the hospital food or the sounds of machines and people that whirred around her.

Ten months is how long Chloe was missing. It was longer than she had thought, and she couldn't remember several blocks of time. This, the therapist said, was a means of survival, and she promised to help Chloe regain her memories from those months.

That's when Chloe refused to speak with the therapist or the doctor about what happened. If she had forgotten blocks of time, she had to believe there was a good reason, and she wasn't eager to remember.

The hospital staff contacted the police the night Gary arrived at the hospital with Chloe. Unconscious and unresponsive, Chloe's bare feet and soiled clothes told part of a tale she couldn't verbalize. Unsure of where

Chloe ran from, the police had to work from Gary's vague recollection of which road he was driving down. The police arrived and waited until Chloe regained consciousness.

Distracted by the bright lights and the repetitive beeping of the hospital monitoring machine, Chloe found it difficult to focus on the questions they were asking. Instead, she would roll over and remain silent, shielding herself with the blue hospital blanket. Chloe had no intention of revealing what had happened. She wanted to put the nightmare behind her and avoid facing the shame that would inevitably come.

As with every examination, Chloe lay motionless as Doctor Scotswood passed the penlight across her unflinching eyes and watched for each pupil's response.

"Looking good," he said. "I'm pleased with how well you're recovering."

Chloe stared blankly into Doctor Scotswood's face.

He flicked off the penlight and tucked it into his pocket before unwinding the stethoscope from around his neck and snapping the earpieces into his ears. He warmed the chest piece with his left hand and then pressed it against Chloe's skin and listened to both her heart and lungs before nodding with a smile.

"I'm just going to take your pulse now." Doctor Scotswood gently lifted Chloe's arm and noted the sturdy pulse that coursed through her veins.

Every time that he examined Chloe, he spoke in a low, calming voice, hoping it would entice her to speak, but never rushing her to do so. He recognized the signs of abuse more easily than many of his counterparts in the hospital, this courtesy of his cruel ex-brother-in-law.

He tucked the bedsheet around Chloe's body and smiled, "You know only a few patients call me Doctor Scotswood, mostly it's Doctor Greg or Scots." His hands folded in front of his body as he leaned forward. "You can call me whatever you're comfortable with, and whenever you're ready, just push that buzzer. Okay?"

Any other time, Chloe would have responded to Doctor Scotswood's kindness. His soft brown eyes, edged with lines that stretched to his hairline, gave him a friendly, not aged look. He cut his black hair in a tapered style, brushed to the side, and held it in place with a pomade that smelled of cedarwood and reminded Chloe of her grandfather. She enjoyed his clipped, rolling South African accent and, although she wasn't ready to talk, she enjoyed listening to him speak. He was neither pushy nor rushed and Chloe knew that if she was going to speak, Doctor Scotswood would be someone she'd feel comfortable talking to. She didn't know why, exactly, but she sensed he knew what she had been through and he understood her pain would take time to heal.

Chloe opened her mouth and then quickly pushed her lips together and smiled. And for the first time, she attempted to communicate, but only with a small nod.

"Well," Doctor Scotswood beamed with a smile. "That's a good start."

He turned to the nurse who was standing beside him and left his instructions for Chloe's IV bag and evening medication.

"Oh, and please leave the bandages off her feet tonight. Her cuts are healing well, and I want to make sure we monitor those nasty stitches before they come out in a few days."

"Sure thing." the nurse lifted the bottom of the bedsheet as Doctor Scotswood left Chloe's room.

The nurse gently unwound the muslin bandages and hummed a soft tune as she cleaned Chloe's wounds. There wasn't a name for the song, it was just something that Julie found calmed her patients. And even though the young girl laying in the bed hadn't spoken to her yet, she could sense that she needed the calmness.

"All done," Julie said as she covered Chloe's feet with the light cotton sheet. "Buzz if you need anything."

But Julie knew that Chloe probably wouldn't use the buzzer or call for help if she needed it. Julie knew it would take time.

Chloe waited until the nurse closed the door before she released a long exhale and relaxed her shoulders. She could hear Julie speaking with the cleaner in the hall as she asked him to remove the garbage from behind the main desk area. A few moments later, the hall fell silent, and Chloe closed her eyes.

Chloe was almost asleep when the slap of his cold skin against her mouth frightened her awake and sent a shiver up her spine. She choked back her scream when she looked into his face. She hadn't heard the door open or his footsteps as he rushed up beside her bed.

His eyes darted nervously from Chloe's bed to the door, and he leaned close, his forehead almost touching hers.

"I'll give you this, you're persistent."

Chloe twisted her head as she tried, but failed, to free herself from his grip. The sticky mustiness of his skin was sinking past her lips and made her feel sick. He held down her right arm with his free hand and Chloe continued to struggle, her muffled screams now fighting to be heard.

"You got lucky, but if you say anything to the cops or that nosey doctor, it won't be you we come after," a sly grin stretched across his lips. "Remember how we found you? We know all about your family, and if you don't want to learn that your poor mama ended up getting hurt, then you'll continue to stay quiet. Understand?"

Chloe's eyes widened at the mention of her mother, and she rapidly nodded her head.

He gave Chloe's head a shove into the pillow before removing his hand and then skulking out of her room. Chloe listened, as the same shuffling footsteps that she heard every day for months, eventually fell silent.

Chloe lay motionless in her bed and recalled the evening that she escaped from the barn and immediately thought back to the innocent lives that she left behind to suffer. She felt a rush of guilt and shame.

Her shaking hand reached over the edge of her bed and fumbled around the side of the mattress until she felt the smooth vinyl cable. She slid her hand to the end, wrapped her thumb over the button, and vigorously pushed down.

A bright red warning light flashed above her bed, casting a violent glow over her body. A faint alarm echoed in the empty hospital hallway, followed by a rush of footsteps as Julie pushed through the door.

"Are you alright?" Julie reached up above Chloe's bed and pressed the switch, instantly silencing the alarm and extinguishing the flashing light.

Chloe's voice cracked as she uttered the first few words she had spoken since her escape. Julie recognized the terror in her words, and after she pressed the security alarm, she grabbed hold of Chloe's hand.

"I'm not going anywhere," Julie promised. "I'll wait here until the police arrive."

6

Simon waited patiently as Chloe explained what happened. First about the attack in her hospital room, then the explanation about her escape, and then finally the harrowing tale of her abduction.

Chloe Stuart was like most teenagers. She felt like she was old enough to live her life and wise enough to do it on her own. Unfortunately, Chloe's determination to be independent and free from her mother's strict rules led her to seek shelter on the streets when she felt she had no choice but to run away.

Thelma Stuart was a single mother, widowed at twenty-one, and left to raise her young daughter alone. A tight-knit community and generous church congregation helped subsidize the wages Thelma earned working in the kitchen at a local restaurant and taking on odd catering jobs, helping her provide a safe and comfortable home for her daughter.

Chloe was a rambunctious, active child that excelled in both school and sports. In her final year of high school, the University of British Columbia offered Chloe a basketball scholarship, but she turned it down instead to satisfy her desire to travel. Years of building dreams and a safe home prompted the argument that Thelma started.

Selfish. Spoiled. Ungrateful. All words that Thelma could never take back and that also pushed Chloe out the door that one fateful day.

Stubbornness kept them apart.

"I was stupid to trust them," Chloe spoke softly through her tears. "I just didn't know what else to do, and I didn't think I could go home."

A lump clogged Simon's throat, and he pushed down his shaking voice. It terrified him that his own daughter could possibly find herself in the same position that Chloe had, but he knew all too well that any child could be at risk.

"You did nothing wrong, Chloe," Simon said, for the fourth time that day. "You are an innocent victim and you have nothing to feel sorry for. In fact, you're incredibly brave to come forward after everything you've been through. We're really proud of you, and I know your mother is too."

"Is she coming?" the pleading look in Chloe's eyes made Simon realize just how much she needed her mother, and at that moment, he ached to hold Dominique in his arms.

Simon nodded, "She'll be here soon."

"I just want to make sure she's alright," Chloe said, her voice slightly more relaxed. "When he threatened to hurt her, I became so frightened. That's what made me ask the nurse to call you. That, and the fact I should have said something sooner."

"The truck driver who found you gave us an idea where he picked you up and we're searching the properties in that area for where you were held."

The memory of the stale coffee and smoke flooded back to her memory at the mention of the man who saved her, "I want to thank him, too."

"I'll get his name and number to you later today," Simon pushed back his chair. "Until then, just rest and heal. And if you think of anything else, give me a call. No matter how small or insignificant you think the information may be."

Chloe nodded. Just as she was thanking Simon, the door burst open.

"Chloe!" the cry of her name and the hurried worry on the face of the woman who called out caused Chloe to bolt upright in her bed.

The two women, mother and daughter, embraced after spending such a long time apart. Ten months of

Thelma not knowing if Chloe was alive or dead, and Chloe not knowing if she'd ever experience freedom again.

Simon left them alone and returned to the police department, even though he was eager to rush home and see his own daughter. It was Dominique that Simon was thinking about when he walked through the front doors of the police station, distracted and preoccupied.

A familiar voice called his name and Simon turned to see Wayne standing at the reception desk with Sally.

Simon wrapped his arms around his friend and former boss. "You have no idea how glad I am to see you."

Wayne's work with the National Human Trafficking Task Force had taken him away from Lake Pines. Between working on several cases across the country, and returning to Lake Pines intermittently to close off his files, Wayne was feeling more nomadic than he was comfortable with.

"Whoa! I've only been gone a few weeks."

"A few weeks too many," Sally added. "We miss you around here Wayne."

"Don't go swelling his head with lies, Sally," Simon joked. "He'll never get out the door."

"Do you have any of that horrible coffee you're famous for?" Wayne asked as he followed Simon into his office.

"Sure thing."

Simon filled two mugs, leaving Wayne's black, and returned to his office where Wayne was sitting.

"I didn't think I was going to see you until tomorrow afternoon. Oliver is eager to have that woodstove installed." Simon handed a mug to Wayne and then closed the door to his office.

"How has it been having him live with you?"

"Truthfully?" Simon asked. "It's been great. Kerry is more relaxed leaving Dominique with her dad, and Oliver has been so amazing with her we have no complaints. He's even joked that he'll have her reading by the time she's three."

"Maybe he can help you?" Wayne laughed.

"Maybe." Simon leaned back in his chair and recognized his friend's serious gaze. "So, what's the real reason you arrived an entire day early? I know you don't have that much free time on your hands."

"I'm here about Chloe Stuart. Her name landed on my desk."

"That was fast. But just so you know, I have Officer Lukas Holland working with me on that case. I was on my way to meet him if you want to come along."

"Actually," Wayne said and let a long pause rest before he continued. "I'm going to be taking over the case entirely."

Simon snapped his body back. "Why? We're perfectly capable of investigating what happened to Chloe. Or don't you think so?"

"It's not that Simon. Over the last year, we've been so close to catching these guys, and every time they seem to elude us. They seem to always be one step ahead and the further ahead they get, the more shielded the entire human trafficking operation gets."

"Chloe landed on our doorstep, Wayne," Simon stabbed his finger on the top of his desk. "You know how incompetent this will make us look?"

"You know that's not true."

"Yes, it will," Simon snapped. "And don't tell me you wouldn't feel the same way if someone came in from Toronto and snagged a case away from you."

"I'm not just some guy from Toronto, I'm working on a national task force trying to break a human trafficking ring," Wayne said, defending himself while trying to make Simon see that what he was doing wasn't personal. "Plus, this is coming from the top."

Wayne pulled out a folded sheet of paper and slid it across Simon's desk. Simon unfolded it and, after reading it, laid it down. The superintendent's signature across the bottom of the official order rendered Simon's protests immaterial.

"I'll have Sally transfer the file we've started to you," Simon said, without raising his face to meet Wayne's gaze.

"Thanks. I'm going over to the hospital tomorrow morning to speak with Chloe and to let her know that there's an entire task force dedicated to bringing these creeps down."

Simon stood, "If there's nothing else, I need to get some paperwork finished before I head home." His words and body language were dismissive. He didn't know when or how it had happened, but at some point, Simon felt like his friend was on the other side of the fence.

Wayne reluctantly stood and walked toward the door. He stopped just as he rested his hand on the doorknob, "You're my best friend, Simon. I'd hate to have this, or any other case come between us."

Simon relaxed his shoulders and nodded his head, "I know Wayne. Me too." But Simon couldn't shake the feeling of embarrassment.

Wayne smiled as he pulled the door open, "See you tomorrow night for dinner."

"You bet."

"And make it good," Wayne joked. "If I'm going to put that woodstove in Oliver's loft, I want to be fed well."

Simon waited long enough to let Wayne make his way through the office and then out the door before he asked Sally to forward copies of Chloe Stuart's file to Wayne. He then informed Officer Holland that Wayne's task force will take over the investigation. Lukas slumped his shoulders in disappointment but said he understood the importance of the task force and offered his help should Wayne or anyone on the task force need it.

Simon returned to his office and pushed Chloe's investigation out of his mind, and spent the remaining part of his day working on the other open files on his desk. However, he still couldn't shake the feeling that he was letting her down.

7

The man behind the glass partition glanced at Kerry, but only momentarily, as she walked through the door. The five waiting room chairs were occupied, four with people and one with an oversized purse. Kerry stepped around the awkwardly placed furniture, over a pair of outstretched legs, and then leaned against the back wall.

Jeremy Turcot had been working in the same clerical position since Kerry first arrived in Lake Pines. He was quiet, efficient, and operated strictly by the rules. Which is what left Kerry with a feeling of unease as she waited her turn to speak with him.

Kerry's purpose for standing in Jeremy's waiting room at eight-thirty in the morning on a Thursday was purely personal. She could not only be reprimanded for overstepping her professional boundaries should she decide to use her provincial credentials to gain information, but she could also lose her job. Her father repeatedly warned her to be careful in her search for

Dominique's birth parents, cautioning that she might not be ready for whatever she was about to learn. As she shifted the weight of her body against the wall, she wondered if she should've heeded his warning. In the end, Kerry decided she owed it to Dominique to learn the truth about what happened to her birth mother and that she'd decide what to do with that information once she had it.

Half an hour after walking into the waiting room, Jeremy waved Kerry over to the counter.

"How may I help you?" he asked, with the faintest amount of enthusiasm as he held his eyes fixed to his computer screen.

Jeremy's mannerisms were the antithesis of friendly. He angled his body away from the reception counter, and he shielded his eyes in oversized tinted glasses as he remained transfixed to his screen.

"I'm looking for some information on a patient of the hospital," Kerry slid her official credentials under the plexiglass partition, and holding her breath she hoped it would elicit some cooperation.

Jeremy glanced at the card and then raised his eyes above his glasses. "The morgue is on the lower floor."

"Actually, she was a patient fifteen months ago," Kerry slipped her identification card back into her pocket. "She was the victim of a hit and run the night an ambulance brought her to the emergency room, which was also the night she gave birth to a little girl."

"It sounds like you have all the information you need on the patient," Jeremy folded his arms, already eager for Kerry to leave the office. "What was it that you thought you'd get from me?"

"I wanted to read her file," Kerry leaned forward on her folded arms. "Just to make sure nothing was left out."

He shook his head, "Unless you have written authorization from either the patient or her doctor, I can't release any information."

Kerry bit her bottom lip and let out a deep breath, "I can't get that."

"Then I can't help you." his response was terse.

"It's really important I see her file," this time Kerry's tone was more pleading. "I won't even leave the office with the file, I'll read it here."

"If it's so important, then get the authorization and I'll release the files."

"But I can't."

"Why?"

"She's dead."

Jeremy stared at Kerry, narrowing his brow, unsure of how to respond.

Kerry rubbed her eyes and ran her hand through her hair, "Look, I haven't been entirely honest with you."

"Really?"

"The girl whose file I want to see is my daughter's birth mother. She was rushed to the hospital the night Dominique was born because she was the victim of a hit and run. I owe that young girl everything, and she may have family that doesn't even know what happened."

Jeremy's demeanor softened, "Why would you risk what you have with your daughter? What if they fight to have her back?"

The question took Kerry by surprise. She had been afraid of that exact thing, but in the end, it was about doing what was right for Dominique. And if she had a father or family that wanted to be part of her life, it wasn't Kerry's place to keep them away.

And that's what she told Jeremy.

"What was her name?"

"Katie Lancaster."

Jeremy turned away and entered Katie's name along with the day she arrived, gave birth, and then died at the hospital.

A few moments later, Jeremy was sliding a printout under the plexiglass partition. "I'm adopted, so I know what a special thing it is that you're doing. Good luck."

Kerry thanked Jeremy and then left his office and read Katie's hospital file as she walked. Most of what she read was exactly what Gloria had already told her. The information that was new to Kerry was what was written at the end of the file.

Anger rose quickly as she read the last paragraph, and Kerry's pulse quickened. She folded the pages and tucked them in her pocket and headed directly to the police station.

* * *

Kerry burst through Simon's office door. Her face was flush with anger and her eyes shouting words she wasn't sure how to speak.

Simon held up a finger and spoke into his phone, "I'll call you back," Simon said as he ended his call. "What's wrong? Is it Dominique?"

"No, well, sort of," Kerry stammered.

She pulled out the folded pages she had shoved in her pocket and handed them to Simon who unfolded them and shook his head as he read it.

"I'm still not sure what you want me to see."

"Look at the date," Kerry stabbed her finger at the sheet.

"It's the day Dominique was born," Simon raised his face from the pages. "Is this girl Dominique's birth mother?"

Kerry nodded.

"Why do you have this?"

Kerry wasn't sure if she saw upset, betrayal, or confusion on Simon's face. She steadied herself as she confessed what she had done and why she wanted to find out who their daughter's birth mother was. Kerry prepared herself for a flurry of protests from Simon, but none came.

"I hadn't realized she died that same day."

Kerry's tears came all at once, "I know I should be happy with the fact we have Dominique in our lives, but I can't help but feel sad that the person who brought her into this world suffered."

"I'm still not sure what you want me to do about this?" Simon waved the sheet of paper in the air.

"The name she gave the hospital was Katie Lancaster, but when the staff tried to reach the next of kin when she died, they realized that the name she gave them was false. Her parents don't even know she died, or that she had a child. And look what the nurse said the police officer's response was when they came to investigate the hit and run."

Simon's jaw clenched as he read the line of text Kerry was referring to.

Possible runaway, no family to contact, and no leads.

"They dropped the investigation!" Kerry snapped.

"I wasn't in the office during that time, I took some vacation time to spend with Dominique after we brought her home. I had no idea."

"But we do now," Kerry added. "So what do we do?"

Simon's phone rang just as he was about to answer, and he held up his finger and asked Kerry to wait.

Simon's face soured when the person on the other end of the line spoke.

"Hi Wayne... yeah, okay... I'll send over the rest of the file later today... okay, bye."

A heavy silence continued for a few moments until Kerry spoke. "That didn't sound too friendly."

Simon briefly explained what had happened with Chloe Stuart's case and how Wayne and his task force were in charge, and Simon and the Lake Pines Police Department were out.

"Don't you think you're being too harsh on him?" Kerry asked. "After all, *that's* his focus now," Kerry said, referring to Wayne's position on the National Human Trafficking Task Force.

"No, I don't. We're perfectly capable of investigating Chloe Stuart's case."

"Think of what Wayne is dealing with. He's trying to save innocent lives. And who's to say that Katie Lancaster couldn't have been one of those vulnerable kids?"

Simon let out a deep sigh, releasing his anger and suddenly feeling guilty for how he reacted to his friend, "You're right."

"Support Wayne because he's your best friend, not just because he's a cop and maybe you can see past your upset at losing a case," Kerry said. "After all, what's more important?"

"You're right," Simon said, feeling the sting of embarrassment. "Thanks for reminding me about that."

"And this?" Kerry pointed to the sheet. "What can we do about this?"

"Let me see what we can do about tracking down who Katie Lancaster really was, and hopefully it won't turn our lives upside down."

8

Two voices, kind and gentle, came from just beyond the slightly opened hospital door. They were soft and low, but Wayne could tell the two people speaking to each other were doing so warmly and kindly. It was how two people who cared about each other spoke.

Wayne lifted his arm, and with a gentle knock on the door, the conversation inside the room stopped. A friendly voice invited Wayne inside and he was greeted with warm smiles.

Wayne stepped forward and greeted the two women who, just moments ago, were huddled in conversation. The first thing that struck Wayne was how much alike the two women looked. Shoulder-length sandy-blonde hair, blue eyes, and a brush of freckles across the bridges of their noses. Chloe was laying in bed, her swollen and bruised feet raised on a pillow, and Thelma perched on a nearby chair. Their arms stretched toward each other and their hands were embraced in a grip.

Chloe, reaching out for comfort, and Thelma, refusing to let go of her daughter for the foreseeable future.

Wayne had witnessed the same scene after successfully reuniting families with missing children. He learned to revel in those moments. That was where glimpses of hope waited in the corners of each smile, and in the swell of their tears. The relief followed intense terror and proceeded years of healing, but it was the sweet spot he chose to gather strength from. They were the missing that hadn't been missed.

However, the moments that cemented Wayne's resolve were the unconnected victims. Those who were rescued from the clutches of human trafficking but had no one to comfort them. With no family looking for them, he wasn't sure how they could ever have been saved without the task force.

"Thelma? Chloe? I was wondering if this is a good time to talk," Wayne asked as he approached the foot of Chloe's bed.

"Yes, of course," Chloe motioned to a chair beside her bed. Across from Thelma's seat. "Is it alright if my mother stays?"

Wayne smiled at them both, "Of course. Family support is essential now."

"The other police officer told me that a task force will investigate my case now. I'm assuming that's you?"

Wayne handed his card to Chloe, who then passed it to Thelma.

"I know this may be uncomfortable, but I need to have you tell me everything that happened. Starting from the point that you left home. I know you are suffering from some amnesia since arriving at the hospital. It's not uncommon for victims to block out painful memories, so anything that you can recall would be a good start."

Chloe's grip tightened on her mother's hand, her knuckles turning a vivid white, as fear and tension built in her eyes.

Thelma placed her free hand on Chloe's arm, "It's alright, Chloe. Tell him everything. You're safe now."

Wayne nodded. "I'm going to need as much information as you can give me and then I promise you I will do whatever it takes in my power to bring these people down."

Chloe closed her eyes. A tear rolled from the corner of her eye and spilled over her cheeks. She took a deep breath and spoke.

Slowly. Carefully. Plodding. Making sure each word was understood and avoiding the need to repeat them.

It had been ten months since Chloe slipped out of her house in the middle of the night. She had a fight with her mother about her future. Thelma wanted Chloe to accept her basketball scholarship at UBC and Chloe wanted to travel and see the world. Harsh words were spoken by each of them and in the end, Chloe decided the only thing she could do was run away.

"I'd still be in my first year at university," Chloe lamented.

"There'll be lots of time for that," Thelma comforted her daughter. "Right now all you need to do is focus on healing."

"Your mom's right," Wayne said. "Part of that healing will come from sharing as much information as you can remember so we can catch these same guys who hurt you."

Chloe dragged the back of her hand over her eyes, wiping the tears away.

"There was this post I found on social media promising jobs at hotels that were looking to fill positions in their restaurants and stuff. It included accommodations, and they'd promised to pay more than minimum wage. Plus, there was a signing bonus if I could start immediately."

"Do you remember the profile or page name?" Wayne asked, but he knew all too well that any trace of the site would be gone.

"I'll look in my account and let you know."

Wayne made a note in his book, "What happened next."

Chloe believed there was no future for her in their small hometown, so the promise of a job at a vacation resort, along with good pay, was worth the trip to meet her contact. She traveled by bus to the nearest city, where a man by the name of Jay was waiting for her at a coffee shop.

"He had a contract for me to sign and I was going to start work at a resort in the Caribbean the next week. I don't even think it was his real name."

Wayne doubted it as well.

"We were having something to eat, and he offered me a drink. We were talking about my duties and where I'd be staying when I felt queazy. That's when I realized he probably drugged my drink. The next thing I knew I was in the back of a truck."

Chloe wasn't sure where she was eventually going to be taken or what either of the men had in store for her, but she realized she was one of the lucky ones. They had used her primarily to pass drugs on the streets and to collect payment from some dealers that Jay and his partner dealt with. However, she realized things were changing quickly when several other captives disappeared and she overheard the two men talking about shipping out the last load and getting new stock.

Wayne cringed at how callously the kidnappers referred to the victims.

"Do you have any idea where they were sending people?"

"No, but I remembered something about where I was being held. The last place I escaped from."

"Great, because our search team hasn't been able to find anything on the road where you were picked up."

"The doctor said I've blocked a lot of memories as a protection mechanism. But last night, I remembered that the building I was in was actually an old barn. There was something about the smell I remembered. Like there was a lot of sawdust on the floor, like a large gerbil cage. They had built these units that were like jail cells inside and that's where they kept us."

"What can you tell me about this barn? Were there any signs or logos that you remember?"

Chloe tried to think back to when she was running away from the cell and toward a door. Trying to recall anything of significance.

"I remember these large metal jugs, almost three feet high. They were along the side of the wall," Chloe said. "I'm not sure if that helps."

Wayne pushed back his chair and pulled out his phone, "More than you realize."

9

He was sitting at her desk when she walked into her lab. His non-descript black suit, cropped hair, and concentrated stare revealed he wasn't a thug who broke into her lab looking for drugs. Not that there were any, but over the years, restless teens had found their way into her lab looking for exactly that, unaware that a coroner had no reason to prescribe pain killers.

"How did you get in here? And who are you?" Kerry reached for her phone and thought that today would've been an ideal day to have brought Raven to work and instantly regretted leaving him at home.

"You can put your phone away," the man stood, buttoned his jacket, and stepped toward Kerry. "There's no need to call Simon."

"How do you know Simon?" Kerry asked. "Or that I was going to even call him?"

"We know a lot about you, Doctor Dearborne."

"Who is 'we' exactly?"

The stranger tilted his chin down, and Kerry was certain she heard a slight chuckle.

"I think you should go now," Kerry insisted, still holding the phone in her hand but not moving to dial Simon's number.

"I'm here because we need your help."

"Again with the 'we'," Kerry said. "Tell me who you are, or leave."

"My name is Ronan Miller," the stranger said, and then more specifically, "Agent Ronan Miller."

"Agent? You don't look like anyone who works with the provincial police."

"Wrong country," the stranger stepped closer. "I'm with the U.S. government. The CIA, to be exact."

Now it was Kerry's turn to laugh.

"Is this Wayne's idea of a joke?" Kerry asked. "Nice, but he could've done better. No offense, but you fit the stereotype a little too well."

"Stereotype?"

"You know, dark suit and cropped hair," Kerry wiggled her finger up and down the length of his body. "All you're missing is a pair of mirrored shades."

"You have this all wrong," the stranger reached into his pocket and flipped out his badge and credentials, and held them out for Kerry to read.

A worried look replaced Kerry's laugh, and she fixed him with a disquietingly intense stare.

The agent folded the black leather badge holder and slipped it into his pocket, "If you want to take a seat, I'll explain why I'm here."

Kerry sat down in the chair next to her desk, and Agent Miller lowered himself into the chair Kerry normally sat in at this time of the day.

"We need your help in identifying a cause of death for someone."

"And by 'we' you mean the U.S. government?" Kerry repeated for clarification.

"Exactly."

"Why would I believe that the U.S. government, specifically the CIA, has come all the way to Lake Pines to have me perform an autopsy for them?"

"Because, Doctor Dearborne, the body is here."

"Then you should call the police department first, and then we'll follow the proper inter-governmental protocols. This wouldn't be the first time an American has died in Canada."

"We can't do that."

"Why?"

"Because only a few people know that this body even exists."

Kerry contemplated what she would say next. Nothing about Agent Miller sitting across from her made any sense.

"If this is so secretive, why even approach me? You definitely have people who can do what I do."

"Yes, but for several reasons, this needs to be kept quiet. And conveniently, you're here and can get to work immediately."

There had been stranger requests in the past, but nothing as so secretive as a CIA agent asking for help to identify a body. In the end, Kerry knew it would be her responsibility to identify a body found in Lake Pines, and reluctantly she knew she'd have to agree to help him.

"I may be crazy, but I'm also curious," Kerry said, acquiescing to Agent Miller's request. "I don't have any autopsies scheduled, so I'll get the lab prepped and as soon as the body arrives I'll begin."

Agent Miller shook his head, "That won't be possible."

Kerry folded her arms across her chest, "Why not? How else am I supposed to examine the body?"

"I'm going to bring *you* to *it*."

Kerry and Agent Miller were locked in an awkward stance. She, uncomfortable with his suggestion, and he, unwilling to make a concession. "I don't think I'm comfortable with that. Bring the body here, and we'll do this above-board."

"We aren't able to transport the body."

Kerry stood and walked around the back of her desk and then turned to face Agent Miller, "I don't think I'm the person who can help you."

"I have a proposition for you," Agent Miller said, switching to an exaggeratedly kinder tone. "You help us identify the body and I'll make sure you get all the information you're looking for on your daughter's birth mother."

Kerry's arms dropped to her side and her mouth gaped open, "How... how do you know what I'm looking for?" Apprehension cascaded over her body, a foreboding signal of something she should avoid, and her father's words resounded in her ears.

"I knew that you'd require the proper incentive to help us, and finding out all you can about your daughter's birth mother seemed like the best way."

An icy chill ran up Kerry's spine. She wasn't sure what she was approaching with Agent Miller, but she was certain that she wouldn't be able to easily step away.

"You can't tell anyone about what you're doing for us either, including Simon or your father. No one can know what you'll be doing, where you'll be doing it, and especially about any of the information you find during your examination. The whole procedure shouldn't take too long and you'll be finished before you know it. We'll get started this afternoon."

Without waiting for Kerry's response, Agent Miller stood and walked to the door, stopping and turning around just before he was about to leave.

"The body is on Airplane Island, which is just south of Sioux Narrows and Whitefish Bay. There will be someone waiting at the end of the road where Schooner Bob's Fishing Camp is, and he'll direct you from there. I left the directions on your desk. Also, if you don't have your own boat, there'll be one there you can use."

Kerry circulated several comments through her mind before speaking, "Where am I supposed to work?"

"We have a tented facility set up on the island and have all the equipment you'll need. We'll be ready to begin as soon as you arrive."

"I didn't say I'd do it."

"You didn't say you wouldn't."

Just before Agent Miller turned to leave, he reached into his pocket and slipped on his mirrored glasses, and stretched an awkward grin across his face. Not quite a smile, however, nor was it a sneer. And before Kerry could change her mind, he turned around and was gone.

10

The afternoon sun was edging over the line of pine trees that partially shielded the small cottage in the center of the island. She raised her flattened hand to her forehead and squinted into the glare, searching for the outline of the dock where she'd tie the boat.

A small wood cabin was built halfway up the hill that reached its peak in the center of the island, directly behind it. An enormous stone fireplace stretched almost as high as the nearest trees, blending almost seamlessly into the branches and leaves that dangled over the cottage porch.

Built near enough to the shore to enjoy the view of the water, but shielded from view from neighboring islands, it was an idyllic setting. Kerry could see how the cottage and island would be a perfect respite for whoever stayed there.

She located the fishing camp and the grim-looking agent who was standing waiting for her arrival, an hour after Agent Miller left her office. The narrow unpaved road looked abandoned with fallen twigs and leaves covering the ground. Unlike the other fishing camp that had signs that dotted the side of the road, Schooner Bob's had no placard or post revealing its location. It was the agent waiting near the side of the road waving that directed her down the right path.

The name, Schooner Bob's, was also out of place on a lake filled with mostly powerboats and small sailboats. The absence of a camp dog was also a dead giveaway that Schooner Bob's was nothing more than a sentinel to whatever it was protecting beyond the shore.

Airplane Island sat in the middle of a cluster of fishing lodges that had been operating in the area for several decades. It was situated only a few miles from the mainland just south of Sioux Narrows and perfectly positioned for privacy. The island had a completely unobstructed view of the lake and was smaller than any of the other islands that Kerry passed on her way from where she started the small tin boat that Agent Miller had left for her.

There was a different feel to this area of Lake of the Woods that Kerry sensed immediately. As she left the small floating dock that was nestled among a thick weed bay, the water slowly cleared as it opened up into the enormous expanse of the Aulneau Peninsula. The shoreline, lined with prairie grass as opposed to the rugged Canadian Shield rock, gave the area a rustic and relaxed feel. The American sport fishermen who normally filled the docks and waterway near the fishing camp that Kerry just emerged from, were only now slowly returning after the end of the global pandemic. Unlike the area closer to Lake Pines which was considered a more typical cottage location, the Aulneau Peninsula and the area of Whitefish Bay retained a quaint lake atmosphere.

Several small cabins that ran mostly without power and were reserved for the rustic at heart, stretched across the shoreline of the peninsula. Largely uninhabited, the islands and land surrounding the area were also a respite for wildlife.

Remaining largely in its natural state and private by location, Kerry could see how, and why, it remained popular for outdoor enthusiasts.

The area was popular among American tourists, and the region's economy depended upon the annual fly-in fishing trips from June to September. Although Kerry had never been on Airplane Island, she had heard the rumors about it being the location where a plane had crashed in a heavy fog that settled on the water following an intense spring storm. The flames engulfed the entire island, destroying all the trees and whatever buildings were on the island, and left no trace or clue as to the number of passengers on the plane. All that remained of the crash was the propellor, which was the only sign that a plane may have caused the enormous fire that destroyed the island.

If the tale was true, the trees had since regrown and a cabin was rebuilt. As Kerry neared the island, the shadowy figures of two men standing on the dock came into focus. Wearing the same black-suited uniform that Agent Miller wore when she found him sitting in her chair in her lab, neither of the men greeted her with a smile as the tip of the boat nudged against the dock.

After Kerry secured the boat and then jumped up onto the dock, the taller of the two men asked for her phone.

Kerry shook her head and placed her hand in a defensive move over her pocket, "I don't think so."

"Don't worry, Doctor Dearborne," Agent Miller said as he sprinted down a set of steps that were carved into the island's rocky terrain. "I can assure you that Agent Christie has no interest in going through your phone. It's just to ensure complete secrecy."

Kerry pulled out her phone and slapped it into Agent Christie's beefy hand with more force than was necessary, and just for extra measure, she let out a sigh. Agent Christie, unfazed by Kerry's apparent upset, turned her phone off and then tucked it into his pocket.

Making eye contact for only a few seconds, before he resumed his guarded position.

"Follow me," Agent Miller waved his hand and turned and ran up the same set of steps he had just sprinted down. His black shoes tapped as they landed on each notch in the rock, making him seem even more out of place.

A glint of light caught Kerry's eye, and she stopped at the end of the dock and noticed a metal propeller that was affixed to the rock face. An edging of small nicks on the lower half of one side of the propeller was the only sign that it may have been in an accident. The prop, now used to hang towels and lifejackets, looked strangely suited for its current purpose, secured to and jutting out of the side of the island.

Kerry pulled herself away from the allure of the prop, and the urge to ask about the tale that was associated with it, and followed Agent Miller up the steps.

Just as Kerry was wondering where on the small island Agent Miller and his team could have set up an area to examine the body, he guided her around a clump of birch trees, and the tented structure came into view. Brown and dotted with blotches of tan and green, the canvas sat over a ten by ten foot area just behind a cabin.

Unlike the dock area, which had two agents standing watch, only one soul guarded the entrance to the tent. A shorter, more pleasant-looking agent greeted Kerry with a nod and a smile as he held open the flap and she followed Agent Miller inside.

It was the smell of the canvas that hit her first. The recollection of the extended tent that was raised in the parking lot at the Lake Pines Hospital during the height of the pandemic flooded back into her mind. The rush of patients into the hospital, some with actual symptoms of the virus and others worried that their allergies or simple cold were morphing into the strange disease that had taken the world by surprise, had overwhelmed the emergency room.

A team of nurses, doctors, and volunteers treated patients as they cried out and struggled to breathe. Inside, the hospital staff was stretched to the edges of their strength, as some survived and others succumbed within hours of arriving. Outside the hospital, it was a different story. Silence filled the space where Kerry worked with two medical students. The calm fell like iron, crushing the comforting quiet that only the presence of the dead could bring.

Trauma. Anxiety. PTSD.

All were resounding effects of the pandemic brought upon the medical staff on the front lines, and Kerry was no exception. She examined strangers and neighbors alike. The elderly and the medically vulnerable took the hardest and initial hits and were among her first autopsies. Eventually, it was clear to see that the virus that triggered the global pandemic held no one in particular esteem. Everyone was a target, and no one seemed safe.

She pushed down the memory of the tent that was used as a makeshift morgue in the hospital parking lot and tried to focus on what she had arrived to do.

At first glance, Kerry could have believed she was standing in a lab, much like the one she worked in for years in Lake Pines. Until she glanced down at the rocks and grass that stretched beneath her feet. An examination table, sink, and a long counter lined with medical utensils and a microscope were waiting to be used. The hum of a refrigeration system reverberated from just beyond the thin wall of the canvas tent and blew cool air through a makeshift vent.

Kerry rubbed her arms, "You thought of everything, Agent Miller."

He smiled, unaware that the slight compliment also came with a tinge of accusation, pointing out the ease of his deception.

"What can you tell me about the deceased?" Kerry asked.

“He died on this island about three days ago,” Agent Miller walked over to the table and pulled back the sheet that covered the dead man.

The man looked like he was somewhere between thirty-five and forty. His short black hair was cropped close to his skull and thin sunglass tan lines stretched from the corner of his eyes to his hairline. He reminded Kerry of the police department’s new recruits. He had a slim build and muscles that were toned but not bulked, and there were no visible wounds, scars, or tattoos.

“We made sure to keep our contact with the body to a minimum when we moved him. And as far as we could tell, there were no outward signs of what killed him.”

Kerry slipped her fingers around John Doe’s wrist and raised his hand and twisted his palm. She then looked up at Agent Miller. “His fingertips have been seared flat.”

“And it was professionally done, too,” Agent Miller explained. “It was a combination of hydrochloric acid and plastic surgery. Normally, the homemade jobs forget about the outer ridges of fingerprints, which can still match up to original prints. But whoever worked on this guy's hands went full circle and removed several layers of skin from around his entire fingertip.”

Kerry lowered the dead man’s hand, “What is it you’re hoping I can help you find?”

"I want to know where he was before he arrived here and, if possible, what killed him."

"Why not start with whoever owns this island?" Kerry asked. "Wouldn't that be the most logical place to start?"

Agent Miller stiffened at Kerry's question, and then ignoring her completely turned to leave, "I'll come back to check on you in a few hours. If you need anything, just ask the officer standing outside."

He left the tent and closed the flap, leaving Kerry alone to figure what killed John Doe.

Perhaps, Kerry thought to herself, it was better Agent Miller didn't answer her question. She had an eerie feeling that it was best not to know.

11

Wayne pushed the last of the five red pins into the area map, growing frustrated with the lack of success he was having in establishing exactly where Chloe Stuart was being held. He used red for the farms that were already searched and yellow for the properties still to be investigated. Officers on his team searched several properties before regrouping in their provisional tactical room at the station. A hush descended upon the group as they watched Wayne strategically separate the remaining farms into quadrants.

He pointed to the farms that the team searched, and suggested a different approach, realizing that besides being lost, Gary Fielding may also have misjudged the distance from town. After dividing up the properties, the officers left to continue their search.

On top of offering one of the vacant rooms in the police department, Simon also assigned Officer Lukas Holland to assist the task force with their search. In the end, the two men agreed it was about the victims and not their egos. Wayne knew that the key to finding the right barn and property lay hidden in Chloe's description of the interior of the barn. The minor features she revealed during their last meeting indicated the barn was used as a dairy farm.

Property and farms that surrounded Lake Pines were spread out great distances because of the large body of water that made up Lake of the Woods. Farms needed to be close to transportation routes, which meant there were only certain areas where the farm could be.

Gary Fielding, the truck driver who found Chloe on the night she escaped, had been traveling along a diverted route because of road construction on the Trans-Canada Highway. The night started out exceptionally dark, and he had been trying to read a map and figure out where he was when he saw Chloe stumble into the middle of the road.

He was vague on his recollection of which rural road he had drifted down. Besides being shaken up at finding Chloe in such a battered state and not remembering the route number or the junction that he turned down, Gary admitted having a poor sense of direction. Something he reluctantly confessed when pressed for details on where he found Chloe. Since he began driving for Baseline North American Trucking, Gary preferred the Canadian route, which was usually straightforward. As opposed to the U.S. routes where he was frequently lost. However, the recent detour had messed with his already poor sense of direction.

Lukas nudged the door open with his foot and walked in unnoticed, while Wayne was deep in concentration and distracted by the map.

"I didn't know if you wanted turkey on rye or a veggie wrap?" Lukas held out two lunch bags wrapped and stamped with Joe Black's Coffee logo on the front.

"What do you think?" Wayne laughed.

Lukas reached in and pulled out the tightly wrapped turkey on rye and handed it to Wayne.

"Any luck?" Lukas nodded toward the map.

Wayne peeled back the clear wrap on the sandwich and took a large bite and shoved it to the side of his mouth as he spoke, "I've narrowed down the farms that either ran or are currently running dairy farms in the area. The most we can go on is how long Gary was driving before he reached the hospital. As well as the fact that he said it was somewhere east of Lake Pines."

Lukas looked at the map as he unwrapped his lunch. A colorful blend of vegetables swirled at the cut opening of his wrap. Red, yellow, green, and tuffs of lettuce and sprouts sprang from the edges.

Wayne caught the aromatic blend of roasted vegetables and balsamic vinegar as he leaned forward and inhaled. “Is that guacamole?” He asked in a curious and desirous tone.

Lukas handed Wayne half of his wrap.

“Do you want to check those five locations out?” Lukas asked, returning their attention to the map.

“I sent two cars out a short while ago. We should hear from them soon.”

“Why did you only pick locations near the highway?” Lukas asked.

“It would be the most likely place for an old dairy farm to be situated.”

“But if it was a derelict farm, it could have been in operation when some of the original train routes were still running,” Lukas grabbed a yellow highlighter and drew a line where some of the original tracks ran. “My grandfather used to take us on hikes along the old tracks when we’d go camping in the summer. He used to work for CN and always loved to tell tales of the times he worked on the trains. We may want to look there as well.”

Wayne and Lukas expanded their search, adding two more farms that were now closed but built where the original tracks ran.

Calls came in from the officers Wayne had sent out to investigate the properties and each time their search came up empty. Not one of the old properties they searched was used to hide Chloe and the others.

This would be the third time that Wayne was within striking distance of capturing a group associated with the human trafficking ring. The last time was three months ago, during a raid just north of Toronto. Additional monitoring of travel and movement of the population during the pandemic not only made it more difficult to place additional members on his task force, but Wayne was also growing frustrated with the ease at which the traffickers could adjust their tactics in how they abducted vulnerable victims.

As with most criminal activities, traffickers modernized their processes, eluding the same authorities that were close on their heels before the global outbreak. Wayne remained undeterred and the task force hired two computer programmers whose sole responsibility was diving deeper into online forums.

Transportation and exchange of victims were a necessary component of the traffickers' business structure. They were just finding different ways to accommodate this, and Wayne was determined to be one step ahead.

"When's that helicopter going to be ready to leave?" Wayne impatiently asked as he looked at the clock, knowing he'd also be losing whatever good light they still had for the afternoon.

"The pilot will be ready to take off in fifteen minutes."

"Let's head over now," Wayne said. "No point in waiting here."

Wayne and Lukas were about to leave when Sally came running down the hall toward them.

"I have a call for you, Wayne."

"Take a message," Wayne said as he grabbed his coat.

"It's Chloe Stuart," Sally said as she held the phone in Wayne's direction. "She said that she remembered something and wanted to speak with you right away."

Wayne dropped his keys on the table and grabbed the phone, "Hello, Chloe? What's up." He was speaking into the phone before it touched his ear.

"I remembered something," Chloe's voice was low and shaky. "I'm not sure if it's important or not, but you said to call if I remembered anything."

"Yes, yes, I did," Wayne said. "Were you able to remember anything about the barn or the property where you were being held?"

An odd looking tree. A lake. A hill. He was hoping it'd be something that could guide him in a specific direction.

"No, nothing like that," Chloe apologized. "It was something I remember overhearing Jay say to the guy he was working with. It was the day after I tried to escape the first time. He had dragged me back to my cell and forced me to take another sedative. But just before I passed out, I remember him saying '*it's a good thing we're shipping this crew out in a week*'."

"Shipping them out?" Wayne asked. "Are you positive that's what he said?"

Chloe sobbed, "I'm sure. I could remember feeling so afraid that if I didn't escape soon, that I may never find my way home."

"Okay, Chloe. Thanks, that at least gives us a timeline to rush toward," Wayne said.

"I'm sorry it wasn't more specific."

"That's alright, remember any bit of information can help," Wayne said. "Just relax and let your mom and the doctors take care of you."

"I will." The two words came out garbled as one, Chloe's nose congested from crying.

He ended the call and placed the phone on the table and stared at the area map dotted with colored push pins.

Wayne took a deep breath and whispered to himself, *just don't let me be late.*

12

The first observation Kerry made regarding the man who lay stretched under the thin sheet on the table in front of her, was that he shouldn't be there. He was young, in his mid-thirties, and had the physique of a man in his early twenties. The calluses on his feet, years hardened into shape, revealed he was a committed runner, and as Kerry assessed his six-foot frame, she also determined it was his primary source of cardio. He was lithe, sinewy, and extremely active. His tightly defined shoulders and back muscles revealed he would be quick to react if he found himself in a fight.

A few small scars edged his palm, most likely from cuts and scrapes he received as a teen. X-rays confirmed he had suffered a broken kneecap and a cracked shoulder blade. But both injuries occurred several years earlier, and could never have contributed to his cause of death.

A small shadow clouded the corner of one X-ray panel and even though there was no damage to the outer layer of skin, a small foreign object sat next to his wrist. She dragged a small blade across the skin, hovering just above the shadow on the X-ray, and pushed back the top layer of skin. A miniature metal square object was implanted and positioned next to the small bone of his wrist. It was too small to identify, but Kerry was certain it was something Agent Miller would be interested in seeing.

She continued her examination, looking for obvious signs of death. There was no gunshot wound, stabbing, or blunt force trauma that could have caused the young man's death. The absence of skin or fibers under the victim's nails also pointed to death free from a physical altercation. At least that's what Kerry could assume. Years of experience told Kerry that she could confirm the cause of his death once she examined his organs, and she suspected Agent Miller had also made the same conclusion.

Knowing that Agent Miller and his team would have already searched John Doe's clothes for any identification, Kerry focused her search on particles, dirt, or traces of substances that could point to a location other than Airplane Island where he had recently been.

Kerry yawned. She suddenly felt a chill in the air. It was more than the cooled ventilation had contributed to the tented space, which meant the sun was setting and the evening chill was rising from the ground below her. It wasn't the dark highway or drive home that was concerning Kerry, it was nightfall on the lake that she was never comfortable with. Shadows and shades of darkness were methods that seasoned lake residents used to make their way safely around islands, rocks, and docks. Traveling the waterways in the darkness, even with a spotlight, wasn't ever something Kerry enjoyed doing.

Without her phone, Kerry could only guess what time of the day it was. She removed her examination gloves, tossed them in the garbage, and then walked out of the tent. She was pleased to see the same young man was still guarding the tent.

"Do you have any idea what time it is?" Kerry asked, placing her hands on her lower back and then arching into a stretch.

"It's almost five o'clock."

Agent Miller was walking up the small hill, "Doctor Dearborne, how did you make out today?"

"If you're asking if I have a name for your victim in there, then the answer's no."

"What did you figure out?" Agent Miller's question was inquisitive and not sarcastic in tone. "Do you have any idea what killed him?"

Kerry shook her head, "I need to bring some samples back to my lab and run some tests on them."

"What tests exactly?"

"I know you only want me to run a basic toxicology screen, but I'll get a more specific picture for you if I test his blood, tissues, and contents of his stomach and intestines."

Kerry watched the look on both Agent Miller's face and the young man standing next to her and noticed they both seemed to lose a hint of color in their cheeks.

Agent Miller composed himself faster than the young guard, "Let's just stick with the initial tests I asked you to run."

"I have all the equipment in my lab. It won't take long and if it makes you feel better, you can have one of your men come with me to watch," Kerry motioned to the man standing next to her. "Preferably this one and not Agent Christie."

Agent Miller allowed a small smile to escape his serious grin. "Alright," Agent Miller agreed. "He'll go with you and bring the results back once you're done."

Kerry turned around and lifted the flap to walk back inside the tent. Agent Miller was waiting when she emerged with a small cooler with John Doe's samples.

"I assume you'll keep the body in proper air-controlled conditions until I return tomorrow?" Kerry asked.

"Absolutely."

"There's just one more thing," Kerry said. "I need to use the bathroom before I leave."

Agent Miller handed the cooler to the young officer and then guided Kerry toward the cabin. The backside of the three-room cabin rested into the side of a hill, leaving one bedroom window level with the ground. They entered through an inside screened porch that ran along the side of the deck that wrapped around the cabin.

The furniture was cozy, not ornate, and had a welcoming and charming feel. Kerry walked past two nautical-themed clothes hooks, a floor lamp with a faded hand-painted shade, and a stack of books as she walked into the cabin. The fireplace mantle was lined with three antique lanterns and an oil painting of two loons hung above them. None of the contents revealed who used or owned the cabin.

"I didn't see any power lines leading to the island," Kerry said as Agent Miller walked her through the cabin and guided her toward the small bathroom.

"You wouldn't have. Propane fuel runs this place and there's a generator when we need a little more power for heat," he explained. "It's fine when the weather is warm, but it can be hard when the season changes."

"You're out here a lot?" Kerry asked, trying to elicit more of a response from Agent Miller.

He smiled and then stretched his left arm out, "The bathroom is just down the hall. I'll wait out here for you."

Kerry closed the door of the bathroom and tried to forget that Agent Miller was within earshot. After Kerry washed her hands, she reached for the small hand towel that hung on the side of the wall. Seven small black and white photos were nailed to the wall. In no apparent order or with any attention to detail. They were personal photos taken on weekend trips to this specific cabin.

They took some pictures on a boat, with fishing gear noticeable in the images. However, most pictures were on the large deck that wrapped around the cabin and in the living area next to the fireplace.

The photos weren't out of the ordinary. Weekend getaways Simon had with Wayne and their friends also produced similar images. Friends laughing, beers in hand, arms around shoulders, and scenes of friends enjoying a weekend together.

It wasn't the images that caught Kerry's attention, but the people in them.

A rapid knock on the door made Kerry jump.

"Is everything okay in there?" Agent Miller asked through the thick pine door.

Kerry opened the door and smiled, "All good."

"Here," Agent Miller held out a small white card and pressed it into Kerry's palm. "Keep this number in case you have to reach someone and I'm not available."

Kerry looked at the card. There was nothing but a number written on one side. There was no logo, name, or official agency print. She was about to ask what emergency he expected she'd be in when he turned around and walked out of the cabin.

She followed Agent Miller down to the dock and retrieved her phone from Agent Christie before she and the second agent jumped into the boat and pulled out of the bay and headed toward Schooner Bob's. The agent guarding her followed close behind in another car. Never falling further than a car length behind. But the entire time Kerry drove, there was only one question on her mind. What did a U.S. Senator and former President have to do with the man who died on Airplane Island?

13

It had been five days since Chloe escaped. Wayne and Lukas helicoptered to the second farm on their list and he hoped they could find the trace of the men who had abducted her. If Chloe's recollection was correct, they were planning on moving the remaining prisoners in a couple of days. However, that had been decided before Chloe escaped. It was likely that her abductors moved sooner than planned, fearing that they'd be caught.

If that was the case, they might already be too late. However, it could also mean in their rush to leave that they left behind a sign or some clue Wayne could follow.

A low beeping sound emanated from Wayne's phone. "We're here," he announced. A blue circle flashed on his screen, marking the location coordinates he entered into his phone's GPS.

Wayne pointed to a property just below. He instructed the pilot to land in the field, placing him as close as he could get to the barn, which was built on the farthest edge of the property. The team he had on the ground was heading toward the same location and would be there within the next twenty minutes.

Wayne grabbed hold of the stabilizer bar inside the helicopter cab and held on tight as they landed.

"Nervous?" Lukas asked Wayne with a laugh.

"You're not?"

Color quickly drained from Wayne's face as the helicopter bounced lightly on the ground before coming to a complete stop. "There are several ways I could go, and this isn't one I'm particularly fond of."

It was the end of summer and there were no signs of the property being used for farming as Wayne and Lukas stepped out of the helicopter and into a field filled with weeds and overgrown grass.

"The farm isn't that old, as far as working farms in the area go," Lukas said as he and Wayne walked toward the barn. "But it definitely hasn't been in operation for quite some time."

As Wayne approached the barn, he withdrew his gun from his holster and held it in front of his body as he reached for the door. Lukas did the same. He dragged the large door open, and slowly looked inside.

It was silent as Wayne shone his light around the darkened space. He called out ahead, walking with measured steps as he made his way through the barn. A swallow flew from its perch on a high beam, disturbed by the open door, and Wayne flinched at the movement. When he realized it was just a small bird, he grumbled in frustration at coming to another dead end.

But as Wayne's light swept over the metal bars and the lined shadows stretched up the back wall of the barn, he cringed at what he saw. They had arrived in a kind of hell and had fallen into a nightmare.

"This is the right place, but we're too late," Wayne sighed. Exasperated at the traffickers evading capture once again. "Let's search the barn. I'll call and request a forensic team to do a sweep of the entire property and see if we can pick up a trail."

Wayne's shoulder's slumped and he let out a painful sigh and then quickly straightened his body. He had to show an unflinching sense of control if he was going to have the men and women who worked on the task force continue to follow him and respect him as their leader.

His eyes followed the glow as more officers moved their flashlights around the barn, absorbing the gravity of what they found. Seeing the conditions where victims were held captive was something Wayne never got used to. The smell and stench of death and desperation were present in every place that he arrived. Unfortunately, like today, sometimes he was too late to save some victims. He cursed as he walked through the barn, recalling Chloe's statement and realizing she remembered more than she realized.

"Thankfully, it seems like they rushed out of here," Wayne said. "They left behind some papers and items that both the victims and traffickers would've touched."

Wayne made note of the clothes, mattresses, and even empty water bottles, knowing they could all be used to obtain DNA samples that could at least help them identify the people they were looking for.

His initial focus was always on identifying the victims. There were the boys and girls who had family looking for them and had reported them missing within hours of their disappearance. Unfortunately, there were the unknown faces who had simply gone missing but were never missed. Those kids were never reported, and until they were found by the task force, no one was aware they were in danger.

The forensic team arrived and cataloged the smaller items that Wayne thought could reveal something about the victims. Videos and photographs recorded the horrific space where the traffickers had kept Chloe and who knows how many other innocent victims.

Time was of the essence. Wayne knew the traffickers would be focused on getting far away from Lake Pines, moving up their original transportation day. The one thing that could be in Wayne's favor is if the traffickers on the other end weren't ready to receive the human cargo. It may just buy him the time he needed.

Wayne left the forensic agents at the barn and headed over the hill and into the valley where the owner of the property lived. Or at least where the only house was situated.

As the evening approached, a cool fog hovered over the ground, giving Wayne all the excuse he needed to avoid the helicopter ride back to Lake Pines. His breath was visible, and he was just feeling the sting of the dampness in his fingertips.

He quickened his pace toward the house and cautiously climbed onto the porch, which looked like it could crumble at the slightest leap. Three cracked railing spindles barely held up the banister, reminding Wayne of an old western film where a cowboy was thrown against a porch in the middle of a fight. He wondered if a similar action caused this railing's break.

His knock on the door was quick and loud, and he waited for what seemed longer than necessary for the door to open.

The old man stood a few inches shorter than Wayne and wore a tattered fleece jacket. The corduroy collar was faded with wear, and a loose thread hung from the left corner. One yank and it seemed the entire jacket would fall apart. His pants were clean but faded and torn. Most likely from previous years filled with farming chores and not hours of balancing on a sagging sofa, which Wayne was certain the old man had just been doing.

Wayne looked beyond the old man's body into the small living space and noticed he was alone. Stale dampness escaped the house the moment the old man yanked open the front door. Anger rimmed his eyes and voice at being disturbed at the end of the day.

Or was it something more?

A blue light filled the dark space of his living room, and a bubbly voice cheered on by a recorded laugh track crackled through the fabric speakers of the old box television set. Wayne wasn't sure if he was more surprised by the fact the old television was still working or because it was playing an episode of Gilligan's Island.

"Are you the owner of this property?" Wayne asked as he held out his badge.

The old man's face didn't flinch, and his head didn't move, keeping his eyes locked onto Wayne's. "Yeah. Who's asking?"

The house, built just beyond the large hill in the middle of the property, was sagging on its foundation. Cracked and faded paint, curled and lifted from the wood siding, had been ignored for years and was now surrendering to the wear of the repeated winters and harsh storms. Rolling hills surrounded the house, completely hiding it from the view of the road, which Wayne assumed was how the owner preferred it to be kept. It's not that the property was large, but the topography made it difficult to see the land in its entirety from one location. Wayne knew it was likely that the man probably hadn't heard or seen the helicopter land earlier.

The old man remained silent. Boring a steely glare at Wayne and then at Lukas. Wayne introduced himself again, this time more forcefully, and asked the old man what his name was for a second time.

"Bruce Grey," the old man snapped. "Why are you asking? And why are you on my property?"

Wayne sensed an unusual nervousness in his tone.

The old man's lower jaw shook, the small patches of white stubble accentuated Bruce Grey's age and frailty, and Wayne thought he looked every minute of his age.

"We have some questions about the barn on your property," Wayne thumbed in the direction beyond the hill.

"What of it?"

Wayne watched the old man's eyes. Lined red with lack of sleep and the remnants of the bottle that sat empty on the table behind him. He was what his father would have referred to as an unsavory character. But was he the mastermind behind the human traffickers that Wayne believed organized in the barn just a short distance from his home? No. But Wayne's instincts told him that Bruce Grey knew more than he wanted to share.

"We have reason to believe that there has been suspicious activity taking place on your property," Wayne explained. "And we need to know who had access to your property, and specifically, your barn."

The old man squinted, his sharp gaze shooting across the threshold, refusing to give up any information. It was, the old man said, his property, and the police had no right to come around asking questions. Poking around in what he said was his 'own personal affairs'.

Wayne tried again with another question and the old man yelled at Wayne to leave his property. And without moving a hand, he shifted his eyes to the rifle leaning against the wall in the house, to amplify his threat. Before Wayne could speak, the old man stepped back into the house and leaned toward the gun. Wayne leaped through the door, stretching his arm forward, and turned the old man around. Then he placed Bruce Grey under arrest.

14

Wayne sat in the chair directly across from Bruce Grey while Lukas leaned against the door to the interrogation room.

The old man looked even more frail than he did when he was perched on the threshold of his house, less than an hour earlier. At that time, he was resolute and determined to not cooperate with the police department, no matter what the issue or the threat to his freedom was.

Now, however, the stare in his eyes was telling a different story.

Bruce Grey stared blankly at the images Wayne was showing him of the inside of his barn. The once-thriving dairy farm looked more like a horror maze constructed for a Halloween event. To hell and back is what it could've been called.

Thick chains lay strewn across the dirty plank flooring, metal cages were secured to the floorboards, and large padlocks dangled from their latches. The vacantness of the cages did little to alleviate the terror that their images generated. And if anyone mistook the cages for animal stalls, the soiled mattresses on the floor would quickly correct that error.

Wayne smashed his palm down on the pile of photographs, "This was happening right under your nose, and you expect us to believe that you didn't know what was happening?"

The old man's lower lip shook and he bit down with his upper teeth, yellowed and chipped, to keep a full shudder from erupting. He opened his mouth to speak, and then quickly pressed his lips together and shook his head.

Then, after an awkward silence, he said, "I know nothing about that." He poked a shaking finger toward the images and then looked away.

Wayne had tried several angles to get Bruce Grey to reveal who had access to the barn. Someone was there, and Wayne was determined to figure out who it was.

After a quick background check, Lukas confirmed that the old man had never been married and didn't have any children. At least none that had been accounted for or claimed by him. Bruce Grey had one sibling, a sister who left Lake Pines when she married a man from Chicago when she was twenty and she has never returned.

"For what it's worth, I don't think you had anything to do with what happened," Wayne said. "At least not directly."

The old man's eyes widened, "What do you mean by that?"

"If you won't cooperate with us and help us figure out who used that barn, then I'll have no choice but to slap an accessory charge on you."

"For what?" Spittle rested on the corner of the old man's mouth as he shouted.

"Human trafficking, kidnapping, endangering human life," Wayne let his words drift, implying that he could find several more charges if he wanted to. However, in reality, he knew that he'd have a difficult time making any of them stick. He just hoped he could scare Bruce Grey enough into cooperating.

"For years the bank's been hounding me," the old man shoved his hands into the folds of his elbow and pulled his arms in close to his body. "Business hasn't been good for years. But I never missed one bank payment, and do you think they gave me any grace when times were hard? No!"

Wayne waited silently while Bruce spoke.

"The farm is all I have, and I wasn't going to lose it, so I decide to rent it out. At first, it was the land I rented out to other farmers who wanted to plant seeds to grow feed for their animals. Then some businesses wanted to store equipment on my property. That's when those guys approached me a couple of years ago."

Wayne sat forward on his chair, "The guys who were using the barn?"

The old man nodded. "They said they were transporting various items across the country and needed a place to store it before they switched trucks."

"You didn't think it was strange?"

"I didn't care, really," he said. "All I cared about is that they were paying me triple what the previous farmer did and they gave me zero trouble."

"Do you have any records of the payments?"

"They paid cash. Upfront for each year in advance."

"So you have no way to prove any of this arrangement," the exasperation clear in Wayne's tone.

"The government has taken enough of my savings. This was a way for me to get some of it back. I didn't care what they were moving, well, at least I didn't care if it was stolen or not. I had no idea they were moving people," the old man's shoulder's slumped forward and for a brief moment, his gaze softened. "I never would have been okay with any of that."

Wayne took down a description of the two men, the old man unable to remember either of their names. The only thing of use he remembered was the make of truck they had driven onto his property.

"It was a bright red Ford F-150 XLT, and it had a white stripe down the middle of the hood and along the sides. It's a '93, I believe, and it was also a stick drive. I could tell by the sound of the engine."

Sally tapped Lukas on the shoulder and handed him a piece of paper with a note from the forensic crew at the barn, "They found something they thought Wayne may want to know about."

Wayne turned around and reached for the paper, just as he did a smile crept across his face. They had both recognized the result of the tests that were taken from some debris on the barn floor. It was the trail they were hoping to find when they arrived at Bruce Grey's farm.

15

By the time Kerry and the agent arrived at her lab, the sun was resting on the horizon.

"Since you're going to be with me for the next hour, or so, why don't you tell me your name?"

"Jack. Jack Graham."

"Alright, Agent Jack Graham, why don't you sit in the chair next to the door," Kerry pointed to the corner. "And whatever you do, please don't touch anything."

Agent Jack Graham was pleasant enough, in fact, he was the kindest person she encountered on Airplane Island. That's not to say he was friendly, and Kerry was certain he wouldn't hesitate to report everything she said and did to Agent Miller.

Kerry tried to pretend that someone wasn't watching as she placed the samples on the glass and slid them under the microscope lens. She recorded her findings and then printed them out.

One by one, she conducted each test through the toxicology spectrometer. A purchase that would never have been approved before the pandemic, but was delivered when the virus was still in its infancy. Fear of the unknown threat the medical community was facing relaxed most budgets that were apprehensive about high-priced testing equipment. But one thing that was agreed upon by all health departments across Canada was the more they knew about the virus, the better off everyone would be.

The hum of the machine filled the silence in the lab and Kerry thought back to the pictures nailed to the wall in the bathroom. Specifically, the two men she recognized in them. Her imagination grew, fueled by the secrecy imposed upon her by Agent Miller and the mystery that seemed to surround Airplane Island. Why else would they have asked her to help with what should be a high-level operation?

Three beeps signaled the end of the tests that Kerry sequenced into the machine, and she waited while the printout recorded the entire findings.

Kerry read the report and knew that Agent Graham was going to leave with both the samples and the printouts.

The one item she didn't need to worry about memorizing was the reading present in the victim's blood. She was certain it would also be present in his bone marrow samples had she taken any.

"Here you go, that's everything," Kerry held out the same cooler she arrived with. This time, packaged with the original samples, any glass slides or trays she used, and the computer printouts from the toxicology report.

"Agent Miller said you'd be back tomorrow morning," Agent Graham said as he tucked the printout report into the side of the cooler. "And he asked me to remind you not to mention anything to anyone."

Suddenly, the friendly Agent Graham had positioned himself sturdily on the other side. Their side—whatever side that was. A simple reminder to Kerry that she wouldn't be able to trust him.

She locked the door once Agent Graham left and returned to her desk, and sent a quick text to her father.

'I'll be home soon'

Kerry suddenly wanted to be nestled in the warmth and comfort of Dominique. Something normal to her, something that was kind. Not deceitful or dangerous, which she was certain Agent Miller was.

Kerry cleared the counter in her lab and spotted the small evidence bag that had been pushed to the side. It must have dropped out as she was unpacking the samples, and it had become hidden under a piece of paper. She grabbed the small piece of metal and ran out of her lab and reached the front door as Agent Graham's rearview lights disappeared around the corner. She was about to call Agent Miller but decided the metal chip, or whatever it was, could wait until morning.

There was just one thing she wanted to do before she left her lab. Kerry did a quick internet search for the toxin she found in John Doe's bloodwork. Kerry was sure he ingested it during his last meal because of the lack of trauma outside his body, and was certain it was how he was poisoned since the toxin would be easy to disguise in layers of flavors and spices. The time it would take for the toxin to take effect would depend upon the amount used.

Whoever poisoned John Doe, did it knowing he'd die somewhere between thirty-six and forty-eight hours.

* * *

Simon couldn't keep from looking at the calendar. Only a few people knew the day was shrouded with pain and deceit. They had suppressed the truth for so many years, that it surprised Simon that he even remembered what day it was. He thought about calling Carly or dropping by unannounced to see his nephews, but something held him back.

He became aware of Carly's secret when he eavesdropped on a conversation she was having with their father. It was years after it had happened, and Carly wanted to confess. She was about to be married and wanted to tell Kenny everything. Their father argued that it would only destroy her life and that it was a secret best left buried.

Simon burst through the door and forced them both to tell him what they were talking about. Reluctantly, his father explained that John Turshen had attacked Carly while she was walking home late at night and that she pushed him over a ridge. His body was taken to a vacant area, buried and forgotten. When Simon pressed for more details and wanted to know who else knew, his father refused to say any more.

"The fewer people who know, the better," was the last thing their father would ever say on the matter, and he died never revealing to Simon where the body was buried.

Even Carly's husband didn't know what the day meant to her. The August day that his sister worked hard to forget was cool and felt close to the edge of winter, just as today felt when he left the house. Simon pulled his phone out of his pocket and scanned for his sister's contact, and then pressed her number.

It rang once when the rapid knock came to his office door.

Wayne opened the door, not waiting for a response, and leaned his head inside, "I think I have a lead on where the kidnappers took the remaining victims, and I'm going to need your help."

Simon nodded and ended the call. He could wait until tomorrow to speak with Carly. At least, he thought, he could give her one more day to forget.

16

"Dirty Ore?" Simon asked. "Like the beer?"

"Not like the beer," Wayne corrected his friend. "The beer is named after what was commonly found in the gold mine."

Samples tested from the gravel found on the floor in a back room of the barn came back as an identical match to a mineral composition from one of the shuttered mines in Lake Pines. The mine, an old gold mine, long since out of commission, held the distinct honor of having been the last mine in the area to end their mining process. Pressure from environmentalists and changing demand in the market made running the mine too costly.

"Dirty Ore was the term given to the gold when it's initially extracted and still encased in rock. The process wasn't pretty, and the rocks brought up—the dirty ore—still needed to be cleaned before processing. Only then could the gold be extracted," Wayne explained.

"The beer, like a lot of the brewery's craft beer, was named after places and myths surrounding the lake."

"Nice to know you're building your knowledge base from our local brewery," Simon joked but was secretly impressed and hopeful that the finding of the dirty ore would lead to the human traffickers and some survivors.

"Thanks for agreeing to come along with us," Wayne said as he and Simon walked toward where their boats were moored.

They had spent several years working alongside each other on cases ranging from petty theft to murder and elaborate drug rings. It felt right for Simon to be working with Wayne again, and he could sense Wayne felt it too.

As they climbed into the boat and pulled away from the dock, Simon glanced over to his friend, who was looking out over the water. "Do you ever miss it here?"

"Almost every day," Wayne admitted, not hesitating to answer.

"Will you ever consider coming back to Lake Pines?"

"Are you worried I'll take my old job back?" Wayne laughed.

"No," Simon smiled and then turned serious. "I just miss having you around. Ever since the pandemic, I really noticed not being able to have my friends close."

Wayne agreed. Travel restrictions kept him away from Lake Pines and made him realize how much he took the area and his friends for granted. His work sent him to provinces across the country and he found he was also missing out on spending time with his brother. Moving to Toronto was supposed to give him more time with Josh, Thomas, and Lucia. His niece had already grown so much in the short time he had been there that he was afraid he'd almost missed her entire youth because of the pandemic and his work. Now there was a bond with Dominique he didn't want to miss either.

Stress had lined Wayne's face. Age certainly added some wear to Wayne's life, but the pressure of the task force and being away from his brother and best friend weighed even more heavily on him.

He hadn't made a formal announcement yet, but Wayne had decided that he was going to retire once he found and arrested the human traffickers who had abducted Chloe Stuart. Even though he would retire from the task force, his enthusiasm for law enforcement was still strong, and he was just going to find another way to pursue that passion.

Plans were already in the works to establish a training academy that would work with both the police forces in the province and private security firms, to train and prepare recruits for service. He would split his time evenly between Lake Pines and Toronto, and hopefully, somewhere in between, he'd find time to settle down himself.

"I had Sally dig out the old mineshaft blueprint and email them to us," Simon's words jolted Wayne out of his daydream. "They'll be able to pinpoint every tunnel and hidden cave in the mine on the island."

Sure enough, as soon as Wayne opened his email, the blueprints to Anchor Island Mine were there. Sally had highlighted the route into the mine from two points on the island and marked the interior spaces where the human traffickers could be hiding.

"We'll want to focus on the area closest to the entrance," Wayne said. "It's not likely that they would have walked too far into the mine if they were using it as a place to wait until they could leave the area."

The police boat bounced over the wave caps as the wind churned up the water. Spray from the waves knocked against the side of the boat, dotted the window, and soaked the front of their jackets. Neither Wayne nor Simon complained.

Four boats pulled up along the natural beach on the east side of Anchor Island, silencing their engines as they landed their boats in the sand. Hand signals replaced words as the group followed Wayne as he guided them toward the opening of the mine.

Following Wayne's lead, Simon and the other officers ran along the overgrown path. The lake on one side and the abandoned mine on the other.

If there was a boat somewhere on the shoreline, they hadn't seen it. Either way, their plan was to assume that they could be ambushed at any moment. There was no way to know how many people were working with the kidnappers. Operations, Wayne learned over his time working on the task force, varied in size.

Even though the overall human trafficking operation was enormous, they counted on smaller-sized operations in rural areas that would abduct vulnerable kids and transport them individually. Working with smaller groups also gave the human traffickers at the top an extra layer of protection between them and the police. It was a process that was simple and effective, but also more difficult to break.

Wayne held out his arm and signaled for the officers behind him to prepare their weapons before they entered the opening of the mine. Overgrown trees hung over the entrance, and rocks that fell and tumbled from the peak of the island cluttered the path inside. A stale stench of animals, both living and dead, hit them as they stepped past the entrance.

Dusty dampness from inside the cave replaced the cool mist that filled the air outside, and with each step, their visibility diminished.

A penlight balanced on the top of Wayne's outstretched gun panned from side to side. His ears were honed, ready to capture the slightest sound that could alert him to any movement around them.

Simon nudged Wayne's elbow and then pointed to the ground. Fresh streaks and footprints on the muddy cave floor veered off to the left.

They followed the marks and spread out to either side of the tunnel. The blueprints indicated the tunnel would lead them to a larger cave fifty feet ahead that measured approximately one hundred square feet. Large enough, Wayne thought, to hold prisoners.

They were thirty feet away when Wayne signaled for everyone to be prepared with their weapons and protective gear.

Twenty feet away.

They could hear the faint sound of muffled voices and feet scraping the bottom of the ground.

Ten feet away.

Wayne would enter first, then the others would follow. Surprise would be their best defense, even if it meant shots being fired in the cave. But Wayne hoped it wouldn't come to that.

Wayne's back rested on the outside of the cave and he flicked off his light and rushed around the corner.

The shout, followed by a scream, came just as the two collided. The young girl squeezed her eyes and gasped. Wayne wrapped his large hands around her shoulders and held her steady as she tried to run. Once he calmed her, her screams turned into sobs. And just beyond the frightened girl who was trying to escape sat two women and one man bound with ropes.

17

He glanced at the floor. Focusing on the restrained captives pushed against the wall. The unmistakable look of fear mixed with surprise flooded all their faces. One by one the officers released the ropes that bound their legs and arms and helped them stand. Their legs were shaky and a nervous worry occupied every movement.

After Wayne instructed the officers to search the mine he guided the survivors to a safe area just outside. The officers returned a short while later, confirming that the two men they were hoping to capture were nowhere to be found.

"At least we rescued these four," Wayne said.

Wayne watched from the opening of the mine as the medical officers tended to the four rescued captives. They were wrapped in blankets and holding bottles of water and being offered protein bars. Their hands shook as they peeled away the silver foil. Wayne wasn't sure if it was because of the dampness in the air or their shock at being free. Probably, he thought, a little of both.

"We need to get these four to the hospital and get them checked out," Wayne instructed. "But I also want them guarded at all times. I'll want to speak with them further about what happened, but for now, let's just let them feel safe."

Everyone agreed that would be the best option.

Until then, there were a few items that his team found during their search of the mine tunnels and caves and they were quickly bagged for evidence. One of the kidnappers left a jacket behind as they rushed to escape and was of particular interest to Wayne.

With a gloved hand, he examined the jacket, searching each pocket, looking for something that may tell him who brought these four victims to the mine.

"Did you find anything?" Simon asked as he emerged from the cave after completing a search of the last tunnel.

"Nothing with a name, but I found this," Wayne held the corner of a piece of paper between his thumb and index finger. "It looks like the corner of a piece of paper. It probably tore off when it was shoved into the pocket."

"Is there anything on it?"

"Just a letter followed by some numbers. It looks like an invoice," Wayne explained. "We'll check it out at the station."

"And the jacket?"

"Did the province let Kerry keep the fancy spectrometer machine thingy?"

"Yeah, she's eager to use it again," Simon said. "I think she's afraid that Peter will call and say she has to give it back."

"I want to have her swab the jacket and see what she can pull off of it. It'll be faster than sending it to Toronto."

"That's not something you hear every day living in Lake Pines," Simon jumped into the bow of the boat and Wayne followed him, the jacket for the kidnapper and suspected human trafficker securely sealed in an evidence bag.

18

The fluorescent lights in the hospital examination room hummed, adding an eerie atmosphere to the room. They rescued three females and one male from the mine. They were dirty, cold, and still shaking with fear. Shock settled in quickly and it didn't seem like it was going to be easy to relieve.

It wasn't a case of hypothermia or even the fright of a car accident. Those were sudden and painful but didn't hold the same horror that these four had experienced.

Jenna Bean was eighteen and the smallest of the four. She had green eyes and short brown hair that looked like it had been recently trimmed. Wayne smiled as he sat down in the chair next to her. A female officer and support worker sat with him and assured Jenna that she was safe and far from the reach of the men who held her captive.

She clawed at the light gray blanket that was wrapped around her shoulders and pulled it tight. Her nails were chewed down to the skin, and her hands shook even though the room was ten degrees warmer than when they first arrived.

"Jenna, my name's Wayne Burgess," Wayne's voice was soft, and he spoke slowly. As eager as he was to capture the men responsible, he was more interested in putting Jenna and the others at ease. He explained who he was and what the purpose of the task force was. He wanted her to know the number of people he had managed to save and return to their families or to the safety and care of organizations that were funded to protect victims such as herself. Most importantly, he wanted to let her know she was safe.

He also shared with her the number of people they were unable to rescue and the urgency in capturing and stopping the men who abducted her. It was important that if she remembered anything about the men who abducted her, that she let him know.

Jenna didn't seem interested in any of the information that Wayne was eager to share.

"I don't want to talk about it," Jenna buried her face in the blanket. "Please don't make me." Her words were low, muffled, and pleading.

She was terrified and didn't want to remember the horror of what she had been through, at least not yet.

"Is there anyone we can call for you?" Wayne remembered the information she gave the first emergency officer who questioned her. "You said your family lives in Calgary."

Jenna's head, still buried in the blanket and shielded from view, bobbed up and down. "My mom and dad."

"I'll call them myself and let them know you're safe," Wayne promised. "Until then, let the nurse and doctor examine you."

Jenna dropped her hands and the blanket fell away from her face. Her eyes flooded with tears and as they fell, they ran traces through the dirt and silt that coated her cheeks. Wayne noticed a thin track of freckles roll over the apple of her cheeks and the bridge of her nose as she sobbed, and Wayne swallowed back his own tears that threatened to come.

"What if they're mad and don't want to see me?" A stressed and worried look crossed Jenna's face, concerned that her parents would be too angry at her for running away to forgive her.

"I can promise you that this will be the best news they receive."

Wayne left Jenna with the nurse, who warmed her with a fresh blanket and the offer of some food.

Ella Logan's eyes glared at Wayne the entire time he spoke with Jenna, and he could feel them burn into the side of his face. He walked across the room and sat down next to her, where she, too, was being comforted by a nurse and a crisis worker.

Ella pushed the nurse's hand away and motioned for Wayne to sit in the chair across from her. She was more eager to speak with Wayne, and he sensed her anger was slightly stronger than her fear. Either shock hadn't set in yet, or Ella was a deeper kind of strong. One Wayne rarely saw in someone so young. Ella was abducted eight months ago after a man befriended her while she was living on the street in Vancouver.

"He pretended to be a runaway too," Ella scoffed at the memory of her abductor, who pretended to be a friend.

He convinced Ella to travel with him to Toronto, where he said he had a cousin who could get them work in a hotel. "You know, one of the fancy one's downtown on the water. He said they also had staff accommodations in the basement."

"What was his name? What can you tell me about him?" Wayne asked patiently, while another officer transcribed every response to his questions.

"I always just called him Jay," Ella explained. "He never told me what his real name was, and to be honest, you got used to keeping a lot to yourself living on the street. You learned everyone had their own story, and you respected their privacy."

Wayne listened while Ella described the abusive house she escaped from and how she found relative safety and security under the Burrard Street bridge. She described a community that looked out for one another and although it wasn't a perfect situation, she never had experienced the betrayal she received from Jay. Ella had no interest in returning home (the word itself made her laugh) and she eagerly accepted the offer to be enrolled in a program that helped kids like her get off the street. However, she worried that because of her age, that she wouldn't be accepted.

Wayne smiled and told her to let him worry about that. "I'll make sure you have a spot."

He watched Ella take in everything happening around her. She was full of a blend of fury, hope, fear, and grace and Wayne realized he'd never seen anyone who seemed so young before. Even though she was almost twenty years old.

"Did you get them?" Ella asked.

Wayne shook his head, "They left the island before we got there."

Wayne left Ella when the nurse returned to clean a few minor cuts she received on the edge of her arm.

He glanced around the room and noticed the doctor was stitching a cut on the teen boy's hand and Wayne moved toward the last of the three girls they had saved.

Amy Hanover was the oldest of the four victims rescued from the mine. Wayne couldn't tell if the side of her face was bruised or smudged with dirt from the cave. As he sat down next to her, he thought it might be a bit of both.

The fear he saw in her eyes when they collided in the mine's tunnel was replaced with the questions she needed to have answered. Where was she? Where was she going to go? But the first question on her lips was the last one Ella asked.

"Did you get them?"

"No, I'm sorry, we didn't," Amy let out a sigh and leaned back in her seat. A nurse struggled to rest an ice pack on Amy's shoulder after she said she hurt it in a struggle. Amy raised her hand and brushed her hair away from her face. "Do you have any idea who they were?"

"I was hoping you could give me some idea. Is there anything you remember about your abductors?"

The vague descriptions of the two men would apply to most men in their twenties or thirties. Amy met her abductor nine months earlier when she answered an ad for a modeling job. She was living just outside of Toronto and moved into the city to strike out on her own and she applied for the job. At twenty-two, she believed it would be the last time she'd have the opportunity.

"They promised me a modeling job with a fashion manufacturer in Asia. He gave me a contract to sign and everything. It looked so official," Amy wiped tears from the edge of her eyes. "I feel so stupid."

"You're not stupid, Amy," Wayne said. "The blame lies solely with the two men who took advantage of you. You're the victim here."

Amy continued with her explanation. She had arrived in Toronto and along with reserving a hotel room, gave her a new set of clothes and a wallet full of cash. When she woke up in the morning, she was in the back of a truck.

Amy covered her face with her hands, "I don't want to talk about what they did, please."

"There will be people who you can speak with, Amy. People who can help you get through this. But for now, I just need to know if you remember names or overheard anything that may tell me where we can find the men who took you."

Amy shook her head and then closed her eyes.

Wayne thanked Amy and then moved over to speak with Russell Becker. He was sitting with his hand wrapped in a thick white gauze bandage, staring at Wayne and eager to speak with him.

"Russell, how are you doing?" Wayne pointed to his hand.

"Not too bad," he wiggled his hand in the air. "And call me Russ, no one ever calls me Russell."

Russ was seventeen and the youngest of the group. Some small-time dealers lured him off the street and offered a job to sell drugs to kids in the city.

"They were pushing pills, pot, just small stuff. But things got sketchy when that Jay guy started coming around."

"Jay? The shorter one with the light brown hair?" Wayne asked.

Russ nodded. "He tried to pretend he was cool and even pretended to understand me, but he had no idea."

Russ said he grew up in an average, middle-class home and had gone to one of the best schools in Victoria. However, even after receiving an early acceptance to a university in the U.S., his teachers still worked against him and were making it difficult to graduate with the marks he needed. The racism he had experienced reared its ugly head when he was within reach of grasping the golden ring he had always strived for. A student had accused him of cheating on his final exams and with no proof, he was given an automatic fail and lost his place at the university. Instead of supporting him, his parents said he brought shame to their family.

In a mix of anger and embarrassment, Russ ran away and found himself on the street. It was only a short time later that he was lured into selling drugs, and when he tried to break out of it and go back home, that's when he was abducted.

When Wayne had finished questioning everyone, he left the four survivors under the protection of the hospital staff where they'd have a warm bed, clean clothes, and care until they could find a safe place to live. Whether it was their family's home or elsewhere.

Wayne emerged from the hospital and darkness had settled over Lake Pines. Clouds clogged the sky, and the wind rustled through the trees. His eyes rested on the faded lights of the small town and their reflection on the water and he knew, when this was over, he'd be returning home to Lake Pines.

19

Simon was sitting at the kitchen table with Oliver. Holding his favorite coffee mug in one hand, and spooning a scoop of oatmeal into Dominique's mouth with the other. Kerry couldn't remember seeing him this contented. Oliver was talking to Raven, who by now conferred with him on all matters relating to food, and Kerry watched from the next room as their morning seemed so normal.

The preoccupation of the toxicology report stole the enjoyment she would normally have had at spending the morning with her family and instead had her wanting to rush out the door after a poor night of sleep.

When she recognized the toxin in John Doe's blood, she thought she had made a mistake and ran the test a few more times.

It wasn't something that could be purchased on the street or found at a local drugstore. Whoever administered it to John Doe did so with the express purpose of ending his life.

Although it wouldn't give Kerry the name of the unknown man, it would give Agent Miller a place to begin his search, and that would mean that Kerry's job on Airplane Island was complete.

Kerry kissed Dominique, grabbed her keys, and headed for the door, "I'll see you tonight."

Kerry had fabricated a story about working on a file that was sent to her by her old boss from Montreal when Simon asked when she'd be home.

"You seem really distracted," Simon said. "Is everything alright?"

Lying to Simon, even if it was by omission, was something he'd see through instantly, and she turned away as she answered. "Everything's fine, just busy."

Agent Miller was clear that she wasn't to share what she was doing with Simon, and after finding the lethal toxin that had been responsible for killing John Doe, she had no interest in putting anyone she loved in danger.

Avoiding Simon was becoming more difficult and his preoccupation with locating the four survivors in the mine was the only thing that kept him from pushing the issue any further.

Simon had sensed that something important was preoccupying Kerry's attention. Neither of them could keep things from each other, and when they brought Dominique into their lives, they vowed to always keep their connection strong and their lines of communication open. And part of that commitment was to never let a lie fall between them. Even the dog was aware of Kerry's distraction and hadn't left her alone all morning.

Simon turned his body around, catching Kerry just before she walked out the door, "I forgot to tell you, Wayne is bringing a jacket by your lab this morning. He wants you to swab it for residue."

"What jacket?" Kerry snapped. How was she going to get out to Airplane Island for the day and avoid Wayne at the same time?

"A jacket we found in the mine," Simon explained. "We think it belongs to the kidnapper he wanted to see if you can get an idea of other places he may have been. It may be a long shot, but I figured with that fancy machine you have, you could find something a lot faster than if he sent it back to Toronto."

"Great idea," Kerry mumbled, not as wholeheartedly as her words implied.

"Is everything alright?" Simon put Dominique's oatmeal on the table and Raven let out a series of barks. Both, Kerry thought, sensing her unease.

"Yeah, just figuring out how I'm going to get everything done today. That's all."

Kerry left before Simon could ask her any more probing questions and she headed for her lab, hoping that Wayne was waiting there with the jacket and that she'd still be able to get to Airplane Island before the end of the day.

* * *

Simon finished feeding Dominique, landing some food on his shirt, and she rubbed her eyes. A sign that they learned was her way of saying she was full.

"Is it alright if I leave all of this mess with you Oliver?" Simon asked, skewing his mouth and giving his father-in-law a wry smile.

"Of course," Oliver laughed.

Simon pushed back his chair, kissed his daughter goodbye, and grabbed his keys.

"Oh, Carly dropped off an envelope for you yesterday and asked me to make sure you got it," Oliver walked over to the hall table and grabbed the sealed envelope that was leaning against the lamp, and handed it to Simon. "You got in late last night, and I was already asleep."

Simon flipped the envelope over and noticed his sister's familiar script on the front. He slid his finger under the sealed tab and ripped it open. When he read what was on the page, all color drained from his face. He looked up, prepared to explain away his reaction when he realized Oliver had already returned to the kitchen and was lifting Dominique out of her highchair.

Simon waited until he was outside before he dialed Carly's number. He wasn't surprised that she picked up on the first ring, he was just surprised by the recent threat that was creeping into their lives.

As he listened to his sister, her voice pitched and frantic, Simon rubbed his hand across his face and let out a sigh.

"You didn't tell anyone, did you?" Carly asked.

"No never," Simon said. "I promised I wouldn't."

"Even Kerry?"

Simon paused, "No, not even Kerry."

20

An hour had passed since Wayne left her lab, and Kerry was just printing the results of the residue tests. Most of what she swabbed on the jacket comprised dust and dirt that matched what was found at the farm and inside Anchor Island Mine.

A smear that ran along the elbow area on the left sleeve was the only area that produced a reading that stood out from the others in the test.

Kerry folded the printout, tucked it into her pocket, and rushed over to the hospital where Wayne had returned to speak with one of the survivors. It was on her way to Airplane Island, and if she hurried, she could be there and back before the middle of the afternoon. And hopefully with information from Agent Miller about Dominique's birth mother.

The hospital kept the four survivors from the mine in rooms next to each other on the same end of the floor where Chloe Stuart was still recovering. Security guards were placed in the hall and only a few hospital staff were cleared to enter any of the five rooms.

Wayne had added Kerry's name to the list and, after showing her identification to the first security guard, she walked over to where Wayne was standing at the end of the hall.

Kerry held out the folded piece of paper, "Here are the test results from the swabs I took from the jacket you found. Most of the results won't surprise you, they just show mud, dirt, and other debris from the farm and mine."

"But you found something," Wayne unfolded the sheet and his eyes scanned the left-hand column. "I can tell by your voice."

"There was a stain on one sleeve," Kerry explained. "It came back as a relatively common lubricant."

"That won't help much, but thanks."

"Well, it's a common lubricant, but it's only used for a mobile harbor crane that's manufactured by a German company."

"Okay, I'll look into this further," Wayne slipped the printout into his pocket. "While you're here, can you sit in with me while I speak with Jenna Bean? I've been waiting for the support worker who was going to sit with us, but she hasn't arrived yet."

Kerry glanced at the clock on the wall. She had texted Agent Miller earlier that morning and told him she'd be delayed by a few hours. As she considered Wayne's request, she knew she could refuse, yet she didn't want to put off what she had to do on Airplane Island.

Kerry agreed, and then followed Wayne into Jenna's room where she was fidgeting with the remote for the television, trying to lower the volume and change the channel.

"I could never get those to work either," Kerry said, eliciting a chuckle from the young girl.

Sitting on an oversized vinyl hospital chair with her feet tucked under her body, Jenna Bean looked younger than her eighteen years of age. Her hair, washed and pulled back with two clips, swept across her neck as she turned her head. Judging by the dark circles and reddened lids under her eyes, Kerry guessed she had slept little the night before.

"I understand your parents are arriving this morning," Wayne said as he pulled two chairs away from the wall. Jenna smiled, eager to see her parents and happy that they wanted to have her back home.

Wayne introduced Kerry and once Jenna agreed to speak with them, he began with the simplest of questions. Jenna confirmed that she had run away from home with a boyfriend about six months ago, finding herself alone and on the street when her boyfriend's parents dragged him home. Jenna was too afraid to call her parents, thinking they wouldn't want her back home.

"Why would you think that?" Wayne asked.

"My parents are super strict. Like mega-strict."

"Is that why you ran away?"

Jenna shifted her body, adjusting the angle in the oversized chair. "They thought I was too young to be dating, and we had been having huge fights about it. They said I was a disappointment, and that I was a bad influence on my younger sister and brother."

Jenna's calm demeanor changed, and as her tears spilled from her eyes, she drew her body closed. Wrapping her arms around her waist.

"They said if I wanted to live with them, I had to follow their rules," Jenna explained.

"So you left."

Jenna nodded and then dragged the back of her hand across her cheeks. Kerry felt a knot form in her gut as she watched the young girl, who experienced more than anyone should have, especially at such a young age.

"Once Ben left, I was alone, and that's when Jay offered me a job and a place to sleep," Jenna said. "He seemed so nice and sincere. I feel so stupid."

"That's how these guys operate. You have nothing to feel badly about," Wayne said. "Remember that."

For the first time, Kerry saw a smile cross Jenna's face. A genuine, relaxed smile. They spoke for a short while longer and Jenna explained what had happened to her during the time Jay and his partner abducted her.

Just as Kerry was wondering how this young girl could have survived such a horrific experience, she noticed a look of surprise flash across Jenna's face as she exploded from the chair.

Lukas had arrived with the two people Jenna had been anxiously expecting. The moment that Jenna saw her mother and father for the first time in half a year, she bolted across the room, and in one fell swoop, they engulfed her in their arms.

Kerry stepped toward the door, paused, then turned around. She didn't see the anger and disappointment that drove Jenna away. What she saw was a mother and a father who would give up their lives and everything they had to be with their child.

Once out in the hall, Kerry could see the mist that was clouding Lukas' eyes.

"Are you alright, Lukas?" she asked.

"Yeah, you should've heard how they were talking about Jenna the whole way from the airport," Lukas sniffed back his tears. "It was just so..."

Lukas's words drifted, but both Kerry and Wayne knew what he was thinking and feeling because they were feeling it, too.

Wayne tugged Kerry's elbow, "I need you for a few more moments."

Kerry followed Wayne, this time into Ella Logan's room, where she was waiting to speak with Wayne. Ella, Wayne said, had been the most forthcoming and eager to speak about what happened. Her anger and fury had strengthened her resolve to do whatever she could to stop Jay and his partner.

Ella smiled when Kerry and Wayne walked into her small room. She was enjoying a double serving of hospital eggs and toast and, unlike Jenna, wasn't waiting for anyone to arrive. She was one of the permanently lost—she was someone who ran away from a horrible life, to only find herself in a worse situation. But she was a fighter, Kerry could see it in her eyes.

Ella reiterated most of what she had the first time she spoke with Wayne, remembering that one man was only referred to as Jay and that they were getting ready to move them somewhere else. To move them into someone else's possession. Ella could speak about what happened to her more easily than the others, and she even shed some light on what happened to other victims. She said she could stay alive on the streets and that gave her the ability to see things that maybe the others didn't see. Either way, Wayne thought both her physical description of the two men who abducted her, along with her accounts of what happened, would not only help the police identify them but that her testimony could help put them away for good.

Wayne's phone buzzed in his pocket and he pulled it out and read Lukas' text, and then raised his face toward Ella. She could see by the look on Wayne's face that he knew she had lied.

21

"Ella Logan is dead," Wayne said, without a harsh tone to his voice, but still with firmness. "Who are you, really?"

The girl they thought was Ella, clasped her hands together and tensed under Wayne and Kerry's gaze. She dropped her chin to her chest and shook her head.

Wayne leaned forward, resting his arms on his knees. "You're not in trouble. We just want to know who you are. I can promise you're safe. You don't have to see anyone you don't want to. I promise." Wayne's words were soft, and he spoke slowly, putting the young girl at ease.

She pushed the curly mound of hair that cascaded over her face and slowly lifted her head. Her large brown eyes looked into Wayne's face and she realized he was worth trusting.

"Ella Logan was a friend of mine," she explained. "We lived together on the streets in Vancouver. She and

I would look out for each other, we would keep each other safe."

"What happened?" Wayne asked. Slowly and patiently.

"Ella either took some bad pills or too much of something, either way, one morning when I woke up she was dead. I didn't know what to do, it freaked me out, and I knew I had to get far away."

"Why did you use her name?" Kerry asked.

"I didn't want to be found."

"What is your real name?"

"Callie. Callie Krueger."

"Callie," Wayne smiled. "You're going to be alright."

Something in the way Wayne spoke, or the way he looked, put her at ease. Callie continued to talk, but this time with hope in her eyes, not just anger.

She wanted to fight back. She said she didn't want to end up like the other girls. Some grew sick, and she remembered one who died. She was aware of two who also got pregnant while they were being held captive. One escaped and the other one gave birth to a little boy. The morning after the baby was born, they both disappeared. Callie remembered the names of every person who was there. She even remembered the names of the ones who she only heard stories about, the ones who came and left before she arrived. Callie vowed to remember every name. Not only so she could help find justice for them if she was ever lucky enough to escape, but so they would never be forgotten.

Wayne patiently listened as Callie listed off the names of the other people who were abducted, along with each fate that befell them. Kerry listened, amazed at Callie's strength. The names were many and their fates beyond sad. But it was the one name that she heard that caused her to gasp.

Wayne and Kerry left the room, Wayne clutching the list of names in his hand, and Kerry with a revelation that met her worst fear.

22

It was mid-afternoon. The police officers had left the hospital and the few family members, who had arrived to retrieve and comfort their children, were planning to return home as soon as the doctors said they were safe to travel.

The five survivors gathered in Jenna's room. It was the first time they were together and alone since Chloe first escaped. They shared their experiences and most of their conversations with Officer Burgess, and Chloe told them about the threat she received in the middle of the night in the hospital.

She, apparently, wasn't the only one.

Russ had also received an unexpected visit and a threat from the kidnapper they knew only as Jay. It was in the middle of the night, and he snuck into his room when the officer on guard wasn't looking. With only a brief window available to him, he told Russ to let the others know they were watching and that they wouldn't hesitate to harm them or their families if the police gained any more information.

Callie grew pale as she listened to Russ. They weren't aware that she had just spoken with Wayne and revealed the names of the other victims and promised to testify against Jay and his partner when they were caught. Callie feared her bravado took her too far and she was just about to admit what she had said to Officer Burgess when she suddenly changed her mind.

She had survived this long on her own and she had no intention of relying on the other four for her safety and security. What she did on her own, was her business and she remained silent.

Then the five survivors looked at each other and made the same solemn vow. They wouldn't say anything more.

23

The young cadet waved Kerry past the construction detour and let her pass through to the side road that would take her directly to Sioux Narrows. A long line of cars stretched back a mile and the delay meant by the time she arrived at Schooner Bob's it would be mid-afternoon. She focused her attention on the evidence bag that felt like it was burning a hole in her pocket, and she pulled it out and dropped it in the middle of her console.

Now that she had the knowledge that it was Polonium that killed John Doe, Kerry was even more uneasy about being involved with Agent Miller. The sooner she handed the bag and the small chip to him, the better.

She had intended on giving it to Agent Miller first thing in the morning, but her delay in helping Wayne meant she had to carry it around a few hours longer. She didn't know what the small metal chip was or if it held any importance. She just knew she wanted nothing to do with it.

What had her mind racing and jumping to conclusions was the photographs she saw in the cabin. She lay awake past two in the morning, trying to forget the image of the man she saw with his arm stretched out across the back of the railing as he relaxed with some friends at the cabin.

But he was no ordinary man, and this was obviously no ordinary cabin.

Kerry pulled out her phone and dialed Simon's number. She had kept this secret from him, unwillingly, and knew that no matter what Agent Miller had said, she needed to let Simon know what she had been doing and where she was going.

She didn't want to have to deal with any of this. Simon's phone rang and Kerry could feel her breathing relax. Once Simon arrived and the entire matter was officially being handled by the police department, she could absolve herself of everything. Even John Doe.

A voice recording instructed her to leave a message, and Kerry disconnected the line. She called the department's front desk and spoke with Sally, who said Simon wasn't in and that she wasn't sure how long he'd be.

"Do you want to leave a message?" Sally asked.

Kerry looked down at the small plastic evidence bag containing the miniature chip and remembered Agent Miller's warning.

"No, I'll keep trying him."

Kerry waited a few minutes and tried again, only to have her call sent to voice mail.

Frustrated, Kerry disconnected the call. It would probably be better to explain everything to Simon in person after she told Agent Miller she was done helping him. She reached the dock and climbed into the boat, and headed through the narrow outlet and toward the island.

The air held a bitter cold that blew through her coat and sweater as she maneuvered the small boat toward Airplane Island. The waves pushed against the bow of the boat, sending sprays of cold water over the edge, narrowly missing her legs. She slowed the boat and steered into the waves, trying to lessen the bounce and spray as she neared the island.

It was the middle of the afternoon, and gray clouds scrambled across the sky in clumps, foreshadowing the first few days of winter. Normally the feeling came in late November, where snow felt imminent and the first few flakes came as no surprise. But it was August and Kerry would rather not be on the lake in a boat when that happened.

Rays filtered through the edges of the clouds, bouncing off the small wave caps and glistening on the surface of the lake. The gleam of the sun reflecting off the edge of the propellor was the first thing Kerry saw as she approached the island. The second was the absence of Agent Christie, which she was thankful for. Once the boat came to a full stop, the small mound of rock at the end of the dock blocked most of the wind, and Kerry's shoulders relaxed. She called out as she climbed the steps, not interested in startling an agent brandishing a weapon.

Water lapped against the shore and the faint song of birds in the distance were the sounds cascading over the small island. Although the atmosphere was peaceful, Kerry ironically found it unsettling. The knowledge of John Doe and the mystery of Agent Miller's presence contradicted the passive nature that surrounded the small island.

Kerry continued to call out as she approached the cabin, climbing the steps to the wrap-around porch. She pressed her face against the pane of glass and peered into the small space inside. The lights were off and there were no signs of movement, not that she was sure what to expect. She gripped the handle and twisted it. It stopped almost immediately. She tried the second door, which was also locked. She turned around and gasped, as the flushed face of Agent Miller was suddenly a few inches away.

"I didn't think you'd show up," his words were breathless, and he leaned forward, resting his hands on his knees as he spoke. "I heard your boat pull up and rushed over."

"From where?" Kerry looked around and could see no viable location from where Agent Miller could have come from.

"Never mind," Agent Miller waved his hand. "I'm glad you're here."

Kerry raised an eyebrow. She hadn't wanted to come and even thought about canceling her trip out to Airplane Island altogether. She couldn't fathom why Agent Miller would be glad to see her.

"I don't know why," Kerry said. "You just wanted me to test his blood for poison and I already did that."

Agent Miller nodded.

"Which is something you could've done yourself," Kerry said accusingly. "After all, Polonium is something your team is quite familiar with. Isn't it?"

"It's actually more of the Russians' flavor of poison," Agent Miller agreed without shock or surprise in his voice at Kerry's tone. "But it wasn't the Russians."

Agent Miller turned around and started down the steps, moving away from the cabin and toward the tented lab behind it. Kerry remained unmoved, and when she realized he wasn't turning around, she reluctantly followed him.

Kerry trailed through the thick bush, pushing aside branches that snapped back in her face.

"Do you want to tell me how you know it wasn't the Russians?" Kerry yelled ahead to Agent Miller, who seemed to keep a steady pace over the rough terrain.

"Because of the chemical makeup of the Polonium," Agent Miller answered Kerry as if she were part of his secret team of agents. Which she had no interest in becoming. "There's a specific blueprint, if you will, for the Polonium that the Russians use and for one that other countries have used."

He pulled open the tent flap and held it back as Kerry walked through. The cold air hit her like a wall, making her miss the dampness outside.

"Why am I here?" Kerry asked. "I already ran the blood work for you."

"I need to know where he was before he died," Agent Miller said, pointing to John Doe who under the sheet, where Kerry had left him. "Can you find out for me?"

Kerry crossed her arms and contemplated her options, realizing she had very few.

"If I'm going to do this, I need more information than you're giving me," Kerry thought back to the photograph on the wall in the cabin.

"Like what?" Agent Miller's gaze was measured, as were his words. Kerry could tell he was deciding how much to tell her.

"You seem so sure that your John Doe here wasn't killed by the Russians. How can you be certain?"

"As I said before, the Polonium you found is not the same chemical makeup that they've used."

"I'm not an expert in political espionage, or whatever it is you're doing here, but I've read enough in the news about the Russians removing former agents or political rivals with Polonium. And for the record, I have no interest in being in their sightlines."

"You won't be," Agent Miller said, with no further explanation. "I told you this has nothing to do with the Russians."

"Then how do you know that whoever used this on John Doe, won't use it on us?"

"Because you're not a threat to that government."

Kerry considered Agent Miller's words and recalled her initial contact with him in her lab.

"You know who John Doe is. Don't you?" Kerry asked. "You never once said you needed to know who he was, you said you wanted to know what killed him. And there's only one way you could be absolutely sure that I'm not in danger from whoever poisoned him. And that's if it was your own government."

The rustling of the canvas interrupted their conversation but hadn't protected them from being overheard.

A woman stepped into the tent and glanced at Agent Miller before she approached Kerry.

"You're only partially correct," the woman was the same size as Kerry, but her athleticism was obvious even through her baggy sweater and jeans. Her dark brown hair was pulled back into a tight ponytail, and her eyes had a sharp focus that held the stare of someone who was always aware of their surroundings in the event they would need to react to a threat.

She introduced herself to Kerry and briefly explained what she and Agent Miller were trying to do. Kerry patiently listened while Serena Davis attempted to make sense of the very odd situation.

One thing, however, was certain. Kerry knew something had happened to John Doe that was of national importance, and even though her instinct was to run away, she also knew it was up to them to find the answer.

24

Simon glanced at his phone and, ignoring the call, silenced the ring and then slipped it into his pocket. He focused, steeling himself for the confrontation that was sure to come. He knew it would be unavoidable. There was no amount of preparation that would make the conversation Simon had to have with Danny Blythe any easier. Or legal.

He knew that just by being at Danny Blythe's front step would be overstepping his boundary as a police officer. Especially if Danny felt the need to lodge a formal complaint against him. However, Simon knew that would be unlikely, considering all the things he knew about Danny.

Simon reached up and knocked on the door of Danny's trailer. Dented, rusted, and resting on a precarious angle, the trailer had been Danny's home as long as Simon could remember.

Rumor had it that the trailer and the property that Danny lived on were owned by an uncle who left Lake

Pines several years ago. The uncle left to work on an oil and gas operation in northern Alberta, and he left the trailer and property for Danny to care for. Which is exactly what he didn't do.

The grass grew in errant patches, filled mostly with broadleaf weeds and discarded cans and cigarette butts. The cracked, hard ground surrounded the trailer and on days where it was raining, a soppy plot of mud led up to the front steps. Dried clumps of mud still clung to the edge of the steps and stained the metal trailer, the remnants of the previous week's storm.

Today, however, was dry and cool, and Simon pulled the top of his jacket closed as the wind tumbled over his shoulders. He couldn't remember an August that was this cold, and he could sense the chill of winter biting at his heels every morning when he left the house. Soon it would be time to pull out the gloves and hats normally stored away until November. The anticipation of experiencing toboggan rides and building a snowman with Dominique was the only reason Simon looked forward to the change of season this year.

Their home, smelling of the scented candles that Kerry always lit at the end of each day and the birch logs struggling for dominance as they roared in the flames of the fireplace, always gave Simon a cozy feeling. Feelings and sensations he knew Danny Blythe could never experience in his dilapidated trailer or with the lifestyle he had chosen.

His home, once a gleaming Airstream trailer with its rounded and polished aluminum body, used to be the envy of several people in Lake Pines. Simon was certain that the manufacturer had never intended for the touring camper to be used as a home for a small-town drug dealer and crook. Although Danny Blythe never escaped suspicions, he managed to elude capture. But Simon knew he needed hard physical evidence if he was going to arrest and charge Danny Blythe with a crime. Instead, both Danny and the police stayed as far away from each other as they could manage.

Danny's name surfaced several times in the last year, often while someone was being arrested. Rumors were spreading that Danny owed a supplier money, and the sum was accumulating interest as product demand waned. Danny was forced to find some cash quickly and wondered if it was his current predicament that brought him into Carly's life.

Simon stretched his arm, reaching up to knock again on the metal door. This time he heard a grunt, followed by the clanging of beer cans falling sideways, echoing from behind the door. Pounding footsteps shook the trailer, already perched precariously two feet above the ground on a pile of crooked concrete blocks.

The door flew open, bounced off the outer frame, and then rebounded just as Danny reached out and stopped the door from slamming closed. His brows folded together as he glared at Simon and then swept his eyes into the field. His shoulders dropped and a smug smirk crossed his face when he realized Simon was alone.

He spat onto the ground, just inches from Simon's boot, "What're you doing here?"

The last two words slurred together and Simon noticed a slight wobble that wasn't spurred on by the unbalanced trailer. Danny squinted his bloodshot eyes and a fetid stench seeped out from the trailer. The door and windows were sealed shut and the aroma of rotting food and spilled beer had taken over the small space where Danny lived.

If it hadn't been for what Danny was doing to Carly, Simon could've felt sorry for him.

"You know why I'm here, Danny," Simon hadn't rehearsed what he'd say. He knew Danny was unpredictable and unreasonable, and he wasn't even sure if he was going to get through to him.

Danny let out a laugh. One that was maniacal rather than jovial, and his thin, pale lips parted, revealing a mouthful of broken teeth.

"So?" Danny egged Simon on, wanting him to say the words that haunted his younger sister Carly for so many years. But Simon wouldn't give him the pleasure.

"Stay away from Carly."

Simon almost added *or else*, but he restrained himself. He remembered what happened the last time he confronted Danny. That was when Danny revealed that he saw what Carly did, and Simon could tell by the look in Danny's eyes that he wouldn't let the issue die.

"What's it worth to you?"

Simon was prepared for some pushback, even a denial. Instead, Danny jumped right to the reason he revived such a painful memory. Money. The sole reason for reaching out to Carly after so many years was to bribe her.

He was in the park the night Carly gave that fateful push to John Turshen. The grove of pine trees cast a shadow over the patch of grass he was sitting on while he waited for a friend to arrive. At first, he thought he was mistaken, and that the several beers he already drank had distorted his vision. But after Carly left, he ran over to the ledge and saw John Turshen lying across the pile of rocks that broke his fall. Danny had always assumed it was Simon who had helped her remove the body from the rocks, and although Carly never revealed who helped her, Simon never corrected Danny's mistake.

"You tell me?" Danny asked. "I know what I saw. You pulled your little sister away just as John took a tumble over the edge and down onto those rocks. I never liked John. He was a sniveling spoiled brat, but I like you even less."

Simon never could get Carly to admit who was with her that night, and in the end, he let the matter drop, knowing that he would've protected his sister no matter what. And if Danny Blythe thought it was him, then maybe he could use it to his advantage and intimidate him into backing off.

If Simon even believed for a moment that Danny would disappear after a quick payoff, he may have considered it. But Simon had met several people like Danny before, and the only thing he could be sure of was his deceit.

"There's nothing to be gained by dredging this up again, Danny."

Danny leaned against the frame and folded his arms together, "I disagree. Plus, it got Carly's attention."

Simon's jaw tensed at the mention of his sister's name.

"Oh, yeah," Danny said. "Didn't she tell you she came to see me?"

Again, Simon just stared into Danny's face, not wanting to give him the benefit of seeing how upset he was.

"I guess she doesn't tell you everything,"

Simon took a step forward, and Danny jumped back. Simon grabbed the front of Danny's shirt, ripping the collar at the seam, and yanked him forward. A wave of protective anger raged in his eyes. He had seen the damage that Danny had caused, and the passing years did nothing to lessen Danny's desire for revenge or Simon's urge to protect his sister.

An image of Dominique flashed into Simon's mind, along with the realization that Kerry knew nothing about Danny Blythe or the threat that hung over Carly's life. A charge of assault would bring unwanted attention to his connection with Danny Blythe and could take him away from his daughter. He knew if he told Kerry about the letter Carly received, he'd have to tell her what happened years before he knew her. Besides not knowing how to explain what happened, he didn't want to explain why he kept it a secret for so long. Simon released his grip on Danny and gave him a shove, pushing down his own desire to scream.

Simon's phone buzzed, distracting him, and he knew he couldn't ignore Kerry's call for much longer. He backed away from Danny's trailer and tucked his hands into his jacket pockets.

"Carly was at least willing to listen. She even offered to consider my offer."

"There's no way we're paying you," Simon seethed. "You've been hanging onto a lie all these years, and you should just let it drop."

"Then why is your sister so keen to work it out?"

"She doesn't want to work it out. She just wants to be done with you. We all do."

Those were the words that Simon shouted, but what he was really saying is that he wished Danny had died in that fire all those years ago. He had blacked out during a night of partying and left a lit cigarette dangling in his hand. A neighbor and dragged him to safety just before his parent's home collapsed. That's when he moved into his uncle's trailer, and his life took a felonious turn. He would've taken his threats, his secret, and Carly's black cloud with him that night. If he had only died.

Danny seemed to understand exactly what Simon meant in his words. What Simon didn't say out loud, he revealed in his eyes. Danny pulled the door shut, the thin glass shaking as the metal door collided with the frame.

Simon's phone buzzed alive inside his pocket, and this time, he pulled it out and glanced at the screen. He pressed the red button and sent the call to voice mail. Kerry could always sense the upset in his voice and he wasn't ready to explain away Danny Blythe or what happened with Carly all those years ago. But he also knew he couldn't lie.

As he approached his car, he dialed Carly's number, and when she didn't pick up, he sent her a text. He needed to speak with her before she tried to speak with Danny again. He wanted to stop her from making another mistake and, hopefully, prevent her from revealing the truth she was so eager to hide.

Simon slammed the car door shut and put the car into drive. He watched in his rearview mirror as the rusted and dented trailer disappeared from view as he rounded the bend in the road.

The truth was lost in a web of confusion and deceit that had clouded his judgment in the past. Simon realized circumstances forced him to become a liar over the last ten years of his life, and he was unsure how to make things right. But he knew he had to try.

25

Agent Serena Davis was a CSIS surveillance officer who worked in cooperation with specific departments in the CIA, most recently alongside Agent Miller. She also insisted that Kerry call her Serena.

There was little Kerry could say, mostly because she didn't know what happened. What she knew was that it was probably a good thing that Simon didn't pick up his phone.

"You're right, we know who John Doe is, but we needed to know what killed him and we didn't have the equipment to do that," Serena said. "And you did."

Kerry looked over her shoulder at John Doe and then back at the two agents, "What's his name?"

"We can't tell you," Serena said. "What I can say, is that you're perfectly safe. In fact, no one even knows we're here."

Kerry stretched her arm out, sweeping it from side to side, "The island or the tent?"

"Both," Agent Miller said.

"We need you to trust us, and maybe when this is all done, you'll understand why we needed to be so secretive," Serena pleaded and then looked to Agent Miller. "Plus, there's something else we need you to do?"

Kerry tipped her head back and let out a deep sigh. What she wanted to do was leave, which is exactly what she told the two agents. When she realized they had no other option, she asked them what it was they needed her to do.

"If you can figure out where he was before he arrived in Lake Pines, we may figure out where he was when he was poisoned and then we can find out who's responsible," Serena seemed to have taken charge in the small tent as she gave Kerry very specific and detailed instructions. "I've read your reports and how useful you were in Montreal and then here in Lake Pines. Plus, the work you did to help during the pandemic was without flaw. This is something I know you can do, then, I promise, you'll be free to leave."

"I'll need to do a more in-depth examination," Kerry explained. "I'll want to use the equipment in my lab for that."

"I figured as much," Agent Miller said. "Take what you need and then test everything at your lab. And as with before, just make sure Agent Graham collects everything."

After both agents left the examination tent, Kerry took samples of John Doe's hair and nails before she examined his organs.

Internal organs, fluids, and tissues would hold clues to what the victim ate and even some particles that he would have breathed. It took Kerry an additional hour to prepare the samples for testing, and as she set them aside on the counter behind her, she stretched her arms, realizing only then how stiff she had become.

She organized the samples in a cooler and cleaned and prepped John Doe's body for storage. However, Kerry wouldn't be surprised if he was gone by morning.

Agent Graham followed Kerry to the lab, as he did the last time, and he waited while Kerry performed the tests on the samples. Patiently, they both watched while the computer printed out the results of the tests. A few hours had passed by the time Agent Graham had left with the repacked samples and the computer results.

As she was clearing the counter in her lab, she heard the front door open and the echo of steps on the linoleum tile in the front lobby. Kerry stretched her head around the corner of the door and smiled when she saw it was Wayne.

"What are you doing here?" she asked.

Wayne held out a cup and a brown paper bag, "I saw your light was on and stopped in and had Lisa whip you up a snack."

Kerry took the food, thanked Wayne, and then took a long drink of the coffee.

"I didn't realize I was so hungry," Kerry confessed. "Thanks."

"No problem," Wayne shoved his hands into his pockets and rocked back and forth on his feet. "I wanted to talk to you."

"What about?" Kerry suddenly noticed the apprehension in Wayne's eyes.

"About today, when we were speaking with Callie."

Kerry nodded.

"You seemed preoccupied, and I wanted to make sure you were alright."

Kerry walked toward her desk and lowered herself into her chair, "I'm fine. It was difficult to hear their stories. Those kids have been through so much."

"It was more than that," Wayne sat down close to Kerry. "It was when Callie mentioned the kids who got pregnant. You looked more than upset, you looked afraid. It was like it became personal for you?"

Wayne watched as Kerry lowered her guard. Over time, he had grown to not only appreciate and respect Kerry as a coworker, but he grew to love her as a friend.

More than a friend, Kerry had become family somewhere along the line. He could tell just by watching her body language if she was happy or upset, and what he saw the moment Callie mentioned the two girls who had become pregnant while being held captive, bordered on the overprotective fear that a parent gets when they worry for their child.

He had seen that same look cross over Josh and Thomas' faces when Lucia escaped their attention for a few moments at the midway while they were at the Calgary Stampede. The three of them frantically began searching for the little girl, Wayne waving his badge to express the urgency in gathering additional help. And Josh and Thomas with terror in their eyes. That was the same look he saw in Kerry's eyes that morning.

Wayne's instincts were good, too good, in fact, to keep her secret from him any longer.

"I've been looking into finding Dominique's birth parents," Kerry admitted. "And I learned that she died the night Dominique was born."

"Oh, Kerry," Wayne placed his hand on her arm. "I'm sorry, I didn't know. Simon didn't say anything."

"He knows about Dominique's birth mother dying, but he doesn't know I'm still searching," Kerry waited for Wayne's reproach, but instead, he offered his help.

"What can I do?"

"She told the emergency room nurse her name was Katie Lancaster, but the officer who was investigating her hit and run said that it turned out to be a false name. And since there was little evidence to go on, and no one had reported her missing, they dropped the case. It's now filed as a cold case."

"When Callie mentioned the name Katie, you wondered if it was the same girl?" Wayne asked.

"I don't know what else to do?"

"Let me do some digging, and I'll see what I can find. It's not uncommon for runaways to use false names or even other people's names, just like Callie did."

Kerry threw her arms around Wayne and thanked him. He blushed and then returned the hug.

"Look, before you get all sappy on me, I also need a favor from you. Can you help me track down Ella Logan's family?" Wayne asked.

"That's the friend of Callie's who died in Vancouver, right?"

"Yeah, I know it's outside my jurisdiction, but I'd like to give them some closure for their daughter."

"Sure thing, but I don't think my government log-in credentials will get me into the files you want me to search through."

“Here, use my info,” Wayne wrote his user ID and passcode on a piece of paper. “That’ll get you where you need to look.”

Kerry took the slip of paper and placed it on her keyboard, “I’ll do some digging before I go home tonight.”

“Thanks, and I’ll let you know what I find,” Wayne said before he left, promising to continue to search for who Katie Lancaster was, and would try to help Kerry find some closure and justice. For Katie and for Dominique.

Kerry welcomed the distraction and began the search Wayne requested. When she finished, she had Ella’s parents' names, both of whom lived in different cities, and also found the missing persons report they had filed a month after she disappeared. Which turned out to be five months before Callie said she had died. Kerry forwarded the information to Wayne and before she logged off, she typed in the three ingredients listed in the contents of the digestive tract for John Doe that showed up on her spectrometer report. The items were just odd enough that she remembered each of them without the need to write them down.

The meal that the victim ate would hold a clue to where he enjoyed his last meal. Kerry was sure it was his last meal because of the stage of digestion. She was also sure it was when he was poisoned.

An internet search for the three ingredients found in the victim's digestive tract took Kerry to some bizarre websites.

It wasn't the presence of pistachios, coffee, or the briny seafood dish that particularly caught her attention. The unique thing about the testing equipment she used for the toxicology report, was how precisely each ingredient was identified. No matter how ambiguous the ingredient might be. In fact, if it weren't for the specific categorization, Kerry would never have heard of a Gooseneck Barnacle or had been curious to search for it on the internet.

She wondered how an ingredient that was normally found in Ukraine could have been paired with a dish that also contained Iranian pistachios and Kopi Iuwak coffee, which was unique, unusual, and found in the Philipines.

Never mind why someone would want to ingest a drink made from coffee cherries pooped out by an Asian Palm Civet, she was more curious how these three items were found in the same meal. However, a restaurant specializing in unique menu items would be the most likely place to search. Which she did, and where she found *Buono.* A seven-table eatery in the heart of Minneapolis. It also would have been an ideal opportunity to administer the poison, unknowingly, to the man who lay dead on Airplane Island.

Kerry grabbed her keys and was rushing to the door when her phone rang. She grabbed her bag and walked toward her car as Lukas described the crime scene. A body had been found washed up on the shoreline, and it looked like murder.

26

Simon pulled off his jacket and tossed it across the back of the chair in the corner of his office. Despite the cold, a layer of dampness coated his body and his face was still flushed with anger. After leaving Danny Blythe's trailer, Simon drove for another half hour, trying to calm his nerves and reach his sister.

For whatever reason, Carly wasn't picking up her phone or returning any of his texts. He left Danny's property with his shoulders pulled back and his gaze steady and straight. However, on the inside, his nerves were jumping and his mind was racing.

If Danny wanted to make the next move, he couldn't do anything to stop him. Several years had passed without a word from him and now, out of nowhere, Danny Blythe was in the middle of their lives again.

Simon was on a fishing trip the night the accident happened, and the only sign that things were different was the sudden departure of Carly. His father, close-lipped about the events of the weekend, had only said that Carly left to spend the school year with their cousins. When Simon pushed for more information, his inquisitiveness was brushed aside. Overhearing the conversation between Carly and their father was the only reason he learned about what happened.

It wasn't until Danny approached Simon one evening revealing what he had seen in the park late that night, that he assumed whatever it was, their father helped cover it up. In not one of his most controlled moments, Simon allowed Danny to goad him into a fight in the middle of the Wet Toad Pub during happy hour. Along with community service, the two boys were told to stay away from each other. Danny was too afraid to go anywhere near Simon, and Simon was just fine never seeing Danny again.

Money problems and deep debt prompted Danny out of hiding when he blackmailed Carly. He pushed the morning interaction out of his mind and forced himself to think of anything but Danny Blythe.

Simon rubbed his eyes and looked at the stack of paper Sally placed on his desk. There'd be at least three hours of paperwork he'd have to finish today, and he decided it would be the perfect distraction.

Many of the backlogged files involved the tickets and charges that were handed out during the pandemic. Businesses that failed to follow gathering rules or individuals who were caught without masks or with groups of people outside their households were given violation notices and then fines that were in line with what Simon was used to handing out to real criminals.

The people that gathered at health rallies weren't members of gangs or felons that were known to the department. They were members of his aunt's bridge club, the local church choir, and Mrs. Mervin, who, at seventy-five, had logged thousands of hours reading to children at the library. These weren't criminals, Simon thought, yet he was tasked with treating them as such.

A rift spread in the community, and Simon knew he'd have to work to mend the hurt feelings and fear that spread during that time.

Simon had no intention of dragging any of these charges out or bringing any of the 'accused' to court. Lake Pines was healing, and he needed to let that happen, otherwise, the virus would have won. File after file, Simon filled the necessary forms to have each charge dropped with only a warning. Sally ensured that each notice was typed, signed, and mailed. By the end of the month, Simon would have each file cleared.

Simon frequently thought about Mrs. Mervin over the past few months. Her warm smile had been relegated to living behind her mask and her cheery eyes had grown tired from the extra effort it took to find joy and hope in being so distant from people she was used to being close to. The vaccines and their mass acceptance allowed businesses to open up their doors, friends were joining again for lunch and walks along the lakefront, and more importantly, people were learning to trust again.

Simon pulled Mrs. Mervin's file out of the stack, "I'll deliver this one myself. I need to mend an old fence."

Sally smiled and offered to get Mrs. Mervin's notice completed before the others. An hour later, Simon was pulling up to Mrs. Mervin's house and walking along her front path. He expected a visual dressing down, and a stern glare just to let him know that what he had done was wrong. Instead, Mrs. Mervin wrapped her arms around Simon and welcomed him into her home.

Fresh coffee was brewing and a warm apple pie was cooling on the counter. When his eyes drifted to the aromatic scents in the kitchen, Mrs. Mervin tugged Simon's elbow and guided him to a seat in the kitchen and together they shared a coffee, a piece of pie, and a laugh.

By the time Simon left, he felt like there was genuine hope for the future of Lake Pines, and the unpleasantness of the morning had faded from his memory.

He was nearing the station when Sally called him and told him Lukas needed him at the base of the grandstand, near the edge of the water just beyond the pier. Simon parked alongside the line of police cars at the edge of the lake. An ambulance was angled between the boardwalk and a pile of rocks that were assembled years earlier as a trial art installation. The town council's art collective referred to it as living art. However, Simon could never figure out what it was supposed to be.

Yellow police tape surrounded an area near the ambulance and a police officer kept the small, but curious, crowd back. Sally hadn't specified what the emergency was but the silence of the ambulance and the officers looking down at the water's edge revealed what had happened.

Lukas raised his hand when he saw Simon and walked over to meet him.

"What happened, Lukas?" Simon asked.

"A couple of runners found a body that washed up on shore," Lukas said. "They pulled him up and tried to help him, but they couldn't find a pulse. One of them performed CPR while the other called the ambulance. By the time the crew arrived, it was obvious he was dead."

"Any idea of who it is?"

Simon followed Lukas, who turned to walk toward the ambulance.

"There wasn't any identification on him," Lukas said. "Just a huge gash on his head. We're going to run his photo and prints through the system and see if we get a hit."

Simon reached the back of the ambulance just as the paramedics were lifting the lifeless body into a black body bag. A knot tightened in Simon's stomach as the zipper was pulled closed. The promise and hope of moving away from the past faded as the cold, blank stare of Danny Blythe glared back at him.

27

Wayne left Kerry's lab and drove directly to the hospital. He needed to buy himself more time, and the more he tried to talk himself out of what he was about to do, the more he could see no other option.

None of the survivors could name any of the abductors, at least not specifically. Just a simple nickname, 'Jay', was the only hint of who the kidnapper was. Wayne hadn't expected any of the survivors to lead a direct path to the kidnappers, clues and evidence would help him do that. But Wayne learned the telltale signs of a lie and a suppression and there was something they were leaving out.

Omission was at the heart of what was keeping him from learning more about the two kidnappers.

Whether intentionally or out of fear, Wayne knew that something was missing from the accounts of the survivors. He just couldn't put his finger on it.

He and the task force had gone as far as they could with the physical evidence they tested, secured, and logged. There were other cases across the country that needed their attention, and he had only a few more days before they pulled him off of the investigation in Lake Pines and sent him to deal with what was happening in other cities. He already had to release the extra officers from his team to attend to a break in their ongoing investigation in Montreal.

Shipping business was picking up in the ports in Montreal after the pandemic, and along with grain and textiles, the flow of illegal goods was also making its way in and out of the country. Unfortunately, human trafficking was also taking place under their noses.

Education and information spread to the public through television documentaries, journalistic investigations, and, most importantly, stories of rescues, all helped bring the awareness of a once-taboo subject to light. A dock worker phoned in a report of some suspicious late-night activity at a pier he thought was closed since the pandemic. Even though many businesses were operating again, much of the global trade had not regained full operational levels yet.

A quarter of the piers had not been in use and the port was working with minimum staff until trade and ports opened up overseas. Workers witnessed trucks arriving in the middle of the night entering a vacant area of the pier with their vehicle lights off.

Port authorities trained nightshift workers to report suspicious activity. Which is what he had done.

Wayne looked at his watch. The team in Montreal would be in place soon and would wait for the unregistered ship to arrive and collect the cargo late in the evening. And hopefully, they could help bring the fight against the human traffickers one case closer to ending.

Wayne could sense he was on a similar precipice of success concerning the kidnappers in Lake Pines. The key was to make sense of the information that the five survivors gave him, and he knew it would point him in the right direction. They were leaving something out, and the puzzle was missing a piece, but he knew there was a grain of truth in each of their stories. They just needed to be connected.

Doctor Scotswood was speaking with a nurse when Wayne stepped off the elevator and nodded to him as he approached the desk.

"I'm just signing the release forms for everyone," Doctor Scotswood said. "I know they're all excited to leave and get on with their lives. They've been through so much and I'm sure they don't want to spend any more time here than necessary."

Wayne rested his arms on the high counter of the nurse's station, "Is there a way we can keep them here a little longer?"

The question caught Doctor Scotswood off guard and he gestured with a shrug and narrowed eyes, "Why?"

"I think they're holding something back, and if we release them now, I'm not sure I'll be able to get the answers we need if we're going to get these guys off the streets."

"You know I can't keep them unless there's a medical reason to do so," Doctor Scotswood said. "I understand where you're coming from, believe me, but I can't legally or morally keep them without a viable reason."

"What if there was a medical reason?" Wayne asked. "Could you keep them here for a little bit longer?"

"There is no reason, Wayne."

"There may be," Wayne hated to lie, especially to the five survivors who had already been through so much. "We think they were exposed to a toxic substance. We found traces of something at the barn that we're still trying to identify."

Doctor Scotswood considered Wayne's words and searched his face for a sign of truth, but Wayne wouldn't make eye contact with him, and in the end, Doctor Scotswood wanted to make sure his five patients were safe.

"I'll keep them for another twenty-four hours," Doctor Scotswood huffed and then pointed a finger at Wayne. "But not a minute longer."

Doctor Scotswood walked away from Wayne and into each room to inform his five patients that they'd have to wait one more day to complete some tests, and then they'd be free to go. Somehow, he felt like it was the worst news he could deliver.

The hospital staff handed masks out to the patients on the fifth floor. And the five rooms at the end, sequestered from the rest of the hospital and guarded by a police officer at the end of the hall, were the focus of the added measure.

Hospital staff had become used to wearing masks and protective gloves full-time, even after the pandemic, but they had all commented on how much nicer it was to treat patients without them.

Russ was the only one who put up a fight when he was asked to wear the mask and remain in the hospital for an extra day. Eventually, he took the mask and slumped down in a chair next to the window, and grumbled something about being treated like a prisoner. Wayne wasn't sure if it was youthful bravado or a young man who was eager to get on with his life and still suffering from the effects of being held captive. Either way, it pained Wayne to keep any of them from leaving.

He just needed to make the next day count as he took down more information from every one of them and tried to find the missing piece to the puzzle.

28

Carly's history became Simon's history. Not just because they were family, but because he knew the secret that connected his sister to the victim of a violent crime.

Lake Pine's most recent murder victim was Danny Blythe and Simon needed to reach Carly before she found out from someone else. Simon knew it wasn't right, but the first reaction he had when he realized it was Danny Blythe being zipped into the body bag was relief.

Relief at not being forced to hide Carly's secret, relief at not needing to speak to Danny Blythe, and relief at not having to face the nightmare that was sure to come. He waited until he was in his car and driving home before he let a smile swell across his face. He sent Carly a text as he was walking into his house and it simply read, "*Call me*".

Oliver was playing in the living room with Dominique while Raven had dragged one of Simon's gloves to his bed by the fireplace, and was resting his head overtop of it.

The unexpected scene brought him an overwhelming wave of happiness.

A knock on the door sent Raven bounding through the living room, over Dominique's play blanket and sliding down the hall.

Wayne was standing on the front step holding a large and poorly wrapped gift for Dominique.

"I hope this isn't a bad time?" Wayne asked, his arms stretched wide around the base of the gift as he struggled to keep it from falling.

Simon moved back, pulling the door open, and Wayne stepped into the hall. The gift, large and oddly shaped landed with a thud when Wayne placed it on the floor.

"Do I want to know what that is?" Simon asked with a laugh.

"Not until Kerry's home," Wayne winked. "I want to see the look on her face when Dominique opens it."

"She won't be home for a while," Simon closed the door and tried to keep any emotion from his words. If there was one person who could see through him, it was Wayne.

"Oh, yeah," Wayne said. "The body found on the shore. Shouldn't you be at the station working on that?"

"I left Lukas in charge," Simon said "He's been keen to work a case on his own, and I thought it would be a good time to let him take the reins. I'll make sure he does everything correctly, but I need to trust my team."

Wayne nodded, recalling the times he left Simon in charge of several cases for the same reason, "Do you know who it is?"

"A guy by the name of Danny Blythe," Simon walked into the kitchen, eager to change the subject, and shouted back to Wayne. "Can I get you a beer?"

"Sure," Wayne, either unaware of who Danny Blythe was or uninterested in taking the conversation further, joined Oliver in the living room.

An hour had passed and Simon had almost forgotten about the afternoon when his phone rang.

"Boss, is this a good time?" Lukas asked.

"Sure, what's up?"

"I'm at the station and I wanted to give you an update on the Danny Blythe investigation?"

Blood pounded in Simon's ears, deafening the laughs coming from behind him. He listened impatiently as Lukas explained everything he had done from the moment he left him at the edge of the water. He wanted to rush Lukas along, hit fast forward on his words, but instead, he nodded and listened patiently.

"We searched his trailer and found a jacket that was left behind in the mess," Lukas hesitated with each word. "It had a tear along the seam and traces of Danny Blythe's blood on the shoulder. There was identification in the pocket. We brought someone in for questioning."

Simon's throat tensed up, and he swallowed as he struggled to get out the next question, even though he knew the answer.

29

Kerry's autopsy revealed what Simon had thought the second he saw the gash on Danny Blythe's head. Someone struck Danny Blythe on the back of his head and killed him instantly. Wood splinters were lodged into the skin on Danny's skull. Lacquered strands of ash, from a shattered piece of wood, edged the fatal wounds where he was struck several times. Even though the police were unable to retrieve the murder weapon, they now knew to look for a wooden baseball bat, broken and cracked where it had collided with Danny's skull. And most definitely would be covered with blood.

Danny's prints and photo image immediately returned a match, and along with it, his address and arrest record. While Kerry was completing her examination, Lukas and another officer drove out to Danny's trailer and searched his property for any evidence that could link him to his killer.

Lukas reported he had found the trailer in the same state that Simon remembered it in. Strewn with garbage and empty beer cans.

Photos of the interior of the trailer were worse than Simon could have even imagined it would've looked like. The few possessions Danny stored in cupboards and drawers, lay strewn across the cracked linoleum flooring. A small table that was secured to the floor, rested on its support at an awkward angle. Everything that would have been on the top was knocked to the floor.

A stained mattress, the edges ripped and frayed, had been pulled from its frame and was resting against a wall, covering a cracked window, the sheets pulled loose and hanging from one corner.

Death, it seemed, came to Danny painfully before the final blow came to his head. The investigative team found no traces of blood in either Danny's trailer or on his property. Except that is for the stain on the jacket.

Something else Simon knew, was that Danny didn't play baseball, and of all the items he had stored in or under his trailer, a bat wouldn't be one of them.

However, of more concern was another item that was found among the mess.

A woman's jacket lay hidden under a pile of debris, and kicked to the corner by whatever confrontation took place inside the trailer.

It was also the reason Simon was walking up the steps to the jail, and not sitting on the floor with Dominique and trying to retrieve his glove from Raven.

Simon extricated himself from any further involvement in Danny's murder investigation; however, that didn't mean he wouldn't be involved. As he signed the visitors' log at the front desk, beside his name and the name of the person he had arrived to see, he just wrote 'family'.

Kenny was just leaving as Simon dropped the pen beside the logbook. He took his brother-in-law in his arms and waited until he was ready to speak.

"I don't understand any of this, Simon," Kenny's voice was muted, but filled with fear and concern.

The first day Carly brought Kenny home to meet their family, the first thing Simon noticed was the clammy sweat that coated his brow. Simon was about to make a joke about Kenny's nervousness, but a nod from his father silenced his words. He looked down at Kenny's hands, already raw with repeated wringing, and instead, he offered him a beer.

Kenny was smaller than anyone Carly had ever dated. He was clean-shaven, short, trim, and had thick curly red hair. A trail of freckles crossed over the bridge of his nose and patches of bright red peered out from where the sun had burnt away the top layer of skin. Soon, Kenny would not only prove he and Carly were soulmates but that he was an amazing father as well.

Kenny pulled away from Simon's embrace and dragged the edge of his sleeve under his nose. He took a deep breath in, and then let a deeper breath out.

"This has to be a mistake," Kenny's voice was pleading and desperate. "I don't know what to say to the boys."

"We'll figure this out," Simon promised, as several scenarios played out in his mind, none included his sister bludgeoning Danny to death. "There must be a simple explanation."

"But the boys?" deep lines edged Kenny's eyes, already bloodshot and raw.

"Keep them home for a few days, and just say that Carly's away," Simon suggested. "I'm sure this will be over before you need to say anything else."

"Keep me in touch, okay?" Kenny asked.

Simon promised his brother-in-law to keep him updated on the investigation and he watched him walk away. Trying his best to be strong for Carly. He turned around and headed to a private room where Carly was waiting.

It was a room Simon had been inside several times before. He interrogated several suspects and took many statements, making sure he exuded confidence and strength. But today, the room seemed small and he felt uncertain about what he could do.

Carly was resting her head on the table, crying into the folds of her arms, and looked up when the door opened.

She couldn't speak when she looked into Simon's eyes, and he had a hard time figuring out what to say first.

"I didn't do it, Simon!" Carly blurted out. "I don't know what I'm doing here."

Simon leaned forward and grabbed hold of his sister's hands.

"I spoke with Officer Holland on the way over here, and it's not just because they found your coat at Danny's trailer," Wayne paused and then squeezed his sister's hand.

"I know," Carly snapped, with more anger at herself than at Simon's comment.

When Lukas drove to Carly's house to ask why her jacket was found in a murder victim's trailer, her face drained of color. She said she didn't know how her coat ended up at Danny's and, then she lied further claiming not to know him. But it was when she folded her arms across her chest that Lukas saw the bruises on her wrists, and the slight scratch that, if she had been wearing a watch, would have covered.

Kerry found small traces of skin tissue under one of Danny's fingernails, and when tested against Carly's, it was a match.

"Why didn't you call me first?" Simon asked.

Carly pulled her hands free from Simon's grasp and folded them over her face. "I don't know!" Her words muffled behind her palms. "I don't know!"

"I tried to call you earlier today, but you didn't answer," Simon said. "Where were you?"

Carly's eyes shot wide, "I was at the park with the boys and I had forgotten my phone at home. By the time we got back, they were starving and I was just focused on getting dinner ready. Before I had a chance to even look at my phone, Officer Holland was on my front step asking about my jacket."

"Kenny was on his way out when I arrived. Did you tell him?" Simon asked.

Carly shook her head.

"You know you're going to have to explain everything to him," Simon said. "Especially if we're going to clear your name and get you out of here. He deserves to know the truth."

Carly agreed with her brother. She knew deep in her heart that Kenny would be there for her, but she was too afraid to reveal that part of her past.

"Did you pay him any money?" Simon asked.

"How did you know he wanted any?"

"I went to speak with him today, and he told me that if I wanted him to go away it would cost me. When I told him I wouldn't pay him a dime, he said that you saw things differently."

Carly lowered her head and admitted that she had gone to Danny's trailer and pleaded with him to stay quiet. She begged him to stay quiet, not for her, but for her boys. They were too little, she said, for them to face such a revelation about their mother.

"That's when Danny said I could make it go away."

"The bribe?"

Carly tilted her head down and nodded, "He grabbed me and tried to drag me toward his bed. We struggled and that's when I pulled away and he must have scratched me. I was out the door, and down the steps when he said there could be another way, and that's when he said I could pay him to stay quiet."

"And you agreed."

"I had no choice," Carly defended. "I just wanted to get away from him."

Simon moved around to the opposite side of the table and wrapped his arms around his sister. He didn't know how, but he'd get her out of jail and have the charges dropped. And if he could, he'd also protect her secret, at least as long as he could.

"There's something else," Carly gripped her lips between her teeth, leaving marks from the repeated nervous habit she picked up when she was a child. She raised her face to meet Simon's. "Kenny doesn't even know what happened. And outside of you and Dad, I only thought it was Danny I had to be concerned about."

A sinking feeling dragged through the pit of Simon's stomach.

Carly leaned forward and whispered, not wanting to take the chance that anyone else was listening. She revealed to Simon what Danny had told her earlier that day. He blurted it out just as she was running from his trailer, angry at Carly's ability to defend herself just moments earlier.

"Someone else knows, Simon. He said it was someone he'd been working with and if anything happened to him, that he had the proof that would put me away."

30

The evening passed quietly, both Wayne and Kerry staying up late with Simon while they tried to figure out a way to help Carly.

"She's also like a little sister to me," Wayne demanded when Simon told him he didn't have to get involved. "There's no way that she killed Danny Blythe."

"I've completed the examination and the autopsy, but whatever I can do, I'll do to help," Kerry wrapped her hands around the mug of tea, trying to stay warm.

Oliver and Dominique had gone to bed hours earlier, and the three sat huddled over the kitchen table with mugs of tea between them and Raven beneath, laying on Kerry's feet. They all wanted clear heads to figure out the best way to help Carly.

"Kenny is turned inside out," Simon explained their brief conversation in the front entrance of the jail. "I didn't know what to say."

Kerry pressed her lips together and looked down at her hands. "You know it doesn't look good Simon?" She asked.

Simon nodded.

"I didn't even know Carly knew Danny Blythe," Wayne said. "He always was a scumbag. Everyone in town knew it, even though we could never pin anything on him. The cops even tried to avoid him."

"Why's that?" Kerry asked, interested about the man who was in the morgue and the reason that her sister-in-law was facing charges.

"He always seemed to slip through getting charged, which always surprised us because he never seemed that bright," Wayne explained. "He always kept his name and hands away from any transaction that could get him in trouble."

"Drugs?" Kerry asked.

"Among other things," Wayne lifted his mug to his mouth and took a long drink. "We think he was also dealing in stolen goods."

"He lived like he didn't have a dime," Kerry said, thinking back to the images of his trailer, tossed and disheveled.

"The only good thing about the pandemic shelter-in-place orders and travel bans was the drop in crimes like robbery," Wayne said. "Unfortunately there was a rise in domestic abuse and human trafficking."

With those last few words, Simon realized he'd be pulling his friend away from his investigation, which was equally as important. As if Wayne sensed Simon's concern, he raised his hand, "Don't worry, I'll have enough time to help you and focus on my investigation."

"How's that going?" Kerry asked. She had thought about the survivors that she sat with while Wayne questioned them. She couldn't help but return to their faces and stories and wonder how they could've survived. Their strength amazed her, and she felt worried for the people Wayne couldn't save.

Wayne shrugged his shoulders, "I think I've hit a dead-end."

He explained his concern that there was information they were leaving out, and had a feeling in the pit of his stomach that he was close. But he was also afraid they were going to get away again.

"What about Bruce Grey? Did you find any more of a connection with him?" Simon asked.

"No, he was completely oblivious to what was going on in the barn. I think the only thing he is guilty of is trying to make some money without reporting it on his taxes. He had been renting out his barn as well as the land on his property, and he was making more money renting out space than he did when he was running his farm," Wayne rubbed his eyes and looked at his watch. "Geez, it's getting late, I'm going to get going."

He pushed his chair back and stood, narrowly missing the dog, who was sprawled out under the table.

"But we're picking this up first thing tomorrow morning," Wayne promised. "We need to get Carly home."

"I already spoke with a lawyer," Simon said. "She thinks she can get her released on bail while the police are investigating Danny's murder."

Kerry put her hand over Simon's arm, "That's good. That'll give us time to find out who really killed him. That's the best way to end all of this."

"Kerry's right," Wayne winked at them both and then yawned. "But for now, I'm off."

Simon cleared the table while Kerry walked Wayne to the door.

"With everything that happened tonight, I didn't have time to thank you for the amazing gift."

Wayne's face reddened at the comment, "I love that little kid, and I just wanted to make something special for her."

"A rocking horse?! That's not just thoughtful, it's incredible. I had no idea you could do woodwork like that?"

"I guess it's all the extra practice I've had fixing up Oliver's suite since Simon obviously can't finish it on his own," Wayne joked.

"I heard that," Simon yelled in jest from the kitchen.

Kerry wrapped her arms around Wayne and have him a tight hug, "We're all lucky to have you, Wayne."

"Yeah, I know."

Kerry waited until Wayne was backing out of the driveway before she closed the door, kissed Simon, and headed upstairs, with Raven close on her heels.

Simon placed the cups in the dishwasher, turned off the lights, and walked up the stairs. He paused at Dominique's door and stood for a few minutes and listened to her low rhythmic breathing. He felt for his daughter the same love and protection he had for his sister. Once Carly was free he would make sure that no one would ever learn what happened all those years ago, and what Danny Blythe had been holding over their heads.

Wayne stopped at the end of the street, waiting for the traffic light to turn from red to green. His car still hadn't warmed up, and he watched a couple run across the street, huddling together trying to keep warm. He had been feeling homesick and spending time with Simon, Kerry, and Dominique was bringing everything to the surface. Hearing that Carly was being held under suspicion of Danny Blythe's murder, brought back the memory from ten years earlier and the hill behind his cabin that held a deadly secret. He couldn't let Carly come this far to lose everything over someone like Danny Blythe and he would do anything to see her freed.

Wayne believed that what he was doing with the task force was important and that many lives depended on him. But he also knew that several amazing officers would continue with those investigations. Training officers to go into the field would allow him to help assemble a qualified team while he returned home.

As he thought of the task force, his mind returned to the investigation that brought him back to Lake Pines. The kidnappers abducted young victims and then transported them to the human traffickers. They worked together and moved too many young, innocent victims through Canada, then out of the country and around the globe.

The traffic light turned green just as the couple reached the safety of the sidewalk and an idea sprang to Wayne's mind. Instead of turning left and heading home, he turned the car in the opposite direction and drove directly to the police department.

Officers working the night shift greeted Wayne as he walked through the doors and headed directly for the office in the back of the station. The late-night comradery reminded him of the early years he worked in the Lake Pines Police Station.

The room, where he and Lukas were working, sat across the hall from his old office. The furniture and placement mirrored the room he spent years working in, making him feel like Alice in Wonderland, however, on the opposite side of reality.

He powered up his computer and logged into the department's database. Lukas had already filed the report for Danny Blythe's murder investigation, along with the evidence they had compiled up to this point. Although there would be several hours of investigation remaining before the case would be closed, Wayne was pleased to see how organized and efficiently Lukas had cataloged the evidence. Wayne smiled and made a mental note to commend Lukas on the work he had done.

Danny's arrest record, although short, had a long list of suspicions and accusations that ranged from his use of and selling drugs to selling stolen goods. His legitimate work record was as unimpressive as his community service. Danny had been unemployed for most of the last eight years, unable to hold down a job for more than a few months at a time.

Wayne read the autopsy report from Kerry's examination, scanning through it quickly since he already knew what the cause of death was. He focused his attention on the photos taken inside Danny's trailer and the surrounding property.

He focused specifically on individual items that were photographed. Most of what the police officers found in Danny's trailer was useless. Junk that was discarded or barely used. Cheap clothes, no jewelry or expensive electronics. For the most part, Danny lived off the grid. What caught Wayne's attention was Carly's jacket with the tear and stacks of paper with numbers and names scrawled across them. Some were full receipts for things like gas and truck parts, and other sheets looked like invoices for larger purchases.

Wayne paused on one image and zoomed in on the top right-hand corner. His jaw dropped open and then he grinned. He hit the print button and then pulled the sheets out of the printer. What started out as an evening of desperation for his own investigation and worry for a close friend, was looking like a night of revelation. And if Wayne was right, by this time tomorrow, he could put everything behind him for good.

31

The sun was just inching over the edge of the hill when Wayne was pulling up to Bruce Grey's house. Although he had already been arrested and questioned, the threat of the police arriving did little to encourage the old man's desire for further cooperation.

"I told you I have nothing more to say to you!" the old man shouted from his porch. The front door swung open and he stormed out of his house as Wayne's car bounced down the uneven path that led from the road to the house.

Wayne held up his hand, waving a small white piece of paper, "Well I have something to ask you."

The old man scowled, a look Wayne was sure he had perfected over a lifetime of use. But there was something else in the old man's eyes. Concern, or maybe worry.

Wayne was now standing on the ground, less than a foot from the front step and he held out his arm.

The old man stared, stone-faced at the sheet in Wayne's hand, and then snapped it away from him. Before Wayne asked the question, the old man's expression had answered it for him. The sheet shook in his hands that were pale and spotted with age.

"You know I have to ask you, even though it's pretty obvious," Wayne said. "Do you know this man?"

Straightening his arm, the old man waved the sheet in Wayne's direction. He slowly indicated with a shake of his head that he didn't know who the man in the photo was.

"You recognize him though?" Wayne asked, more specifically.

This time, Bruce Grey nodded. "Yeah, he was one of the two guys who came to rent the barn."

Wayne let out a sigh, "Did you ever have any contact with him after that day?"

"No, I told you I didn't," the old man snapped, and then, more softly added, "I had nothing to do with those poor kids being taken."

Wayne doubted that Bruce Grey was aware of the kidnapped victims that had been held in his barn for so many months. He even sensed that the old man felt some guilt about that, no matter how sour his disposition was toward Wayne. And Wayne believed it would be the guilt that he'd have difficulty forgetting over the remaining years he had left.

"Did you see or hear from him after you returned from the station?"

The pause after the question was difficult to miss.

"I can just bring you in again if you don't want to tell me now," Wayne waved his hand toward his car.

"He came by right after one of your police officers brought me home. I told him I wanted nothing to do with him or what they were doing and to get off my property."

"Why didn't you call us and let us know," Wayne's anger rose to the surface of his face, and impossible to hide in his tone. Wayne took a step closer to the porch.

"After what I went through? I was terrified."

Wayne could see the fear in the man's eyes, and it had nothing to do with Wayne standing before him.

"He came by looking for the other guy he was with, said they skipped out on some money they owed him. He had been trying to track them down and said they just up and disappeared," spittle accumulated on the corner of the old man's withered lips. "I told him to get off my property and that I thought it was sick what they were doing. He pretended like he didn't know what they were up to. Could you believe it? He denied being any part of what they were doing. He threatened me and said if I told the cops that he'd been around that he'd take care of me."

"What'd you do?"

"Grabbed by rifle and shot it in the air," Bruce jerked his head and grinned. "Told him the next time I wouldn't miss."

When Wayne told the old man that Danny was killed, he looked neither upset nor worried.

"Good riddance." Is all he muttered.

The old man's frail arms and shuffling gait would have made it impossible to overpower Danny Blythe in a fight. And since Bruce Grey proved his preferred method of confrontation involved his rifle, Wayne knew he wasn't the person who would've killed Danny Blythe.

With a warning not to keep information from the police, Wayne turned to leave.

"How'd you know he was here?" Bruce Grey shouted from his porch.

"He had a receipt for some truck parts and they were for a '93 red Ford F-150 XLT."

The old man grinned as Wayne climbed behind the wheel and pulled away from the farm.

He unfolded the second piece of paper he had found in the evidence file. The font type and invoice number on the paper found in Danny's trailer were identical to the small corner of torn paper Wayne found in the kidnapper's jacket. He hoped that this would finally lead him a step closer to the kidnappers, and even prove who really killed Danny Blythe.

Wayne was the last member of the task force remaining in Lake Pines. The urgent call for the remaining officers to return to Montreal left him without backup on the final lead.

Simon was preoccupied with figuring out how to get Carly out on bail and Lukas was proving his worth working on the investigation into Danny Blythe's murder.

Wayne didn't want to compromise either case by calling Wayne or Lukas and telling them what he was going to follow up on next.

It would have been easy to miss the link between the two cases, and if Wayne hadn't been invested in helping Carly he may even have overlooked it.

Danny Blythe's connection to the kidnappers put his murder in a different light, but it was what seemed like a random invoice that connected them both for Wayne.

He had seen too many investigations get thrown off track when an investigating officer finds information, seemingly, out of left-field. And the mention of the truck by Bruce Grey and the secondary invoice did just that.

In case Wayne was wrong, he didn't want to take Lukas or Simon away from what they needed to focus on, and everything was time-sensitive.

Wayne opened up the internet browser on his phone and punched in the information from the invoice. The voice, of someone who Wayne could only assume was the office clerk, announced that the office was closed and would not open until ten o'clock.

He pounded his palm against the steering wheel, frustrated at the lack of access. He was about to call the task force lead in Toronto when he realized that his old boss Peter George, now a superintendent within the provincial police ranks, had a long history of contacts with the police division where he was headed. Plus, it would give him a chance to talk about his planned move.

Peter was preparing for a budget meeting when Wayne called. He was upset to hear about Carly's predicament as well as Wayne's frustration with the kidnappers and survivors.

"I understand the frustration well, Wayne," Peter said. "You need to balance your compassion and understanding for the victims with wanting to bring the criminals to justice. But, having them kept in the hospital under false pretenses wasn't the way to go about it."

"I know, and believe me, if there's any reprimand coming for doing that, I'll accept it easily."

"It could jeopardize your standing with the task force."

"That's the other thing I wanted to speak with you about," Wayne said, buffering his request with an apology. "I just didn't think I'd be approaching you so soon."

Wayne explained his idea of establishing a training academy that would allow him to work out of Lake Pines as well as other parts of the country.

"It's not a bad idea Wayne," Peter admitted. "As a matter of fact, I was talking about that with Commissioner Robertson ever since I transferred out of Lake Pines."

"Do you think he'd go for it?"

"Yeah, I think it would be worth sitting down and talking with him about what you had planned." Peter paused, "when were you planning on leaving the task force?"

"As soon as I close this case. Being back in Lake Pines has made me realize how much I miss being here and I don't want to let any more time pass. I'm not exactly young."

Peter laughed. It had always been a running joke between Wayne and Peter that they seemed so old compared to the other officers they worked with. Everyone except Commissioner Gris Robertson.

"I'll set up a time next week and the three of us can sit down and discuss it," Peter suggested. "Simon must be pretty excited about you moving back."

"I haven't told him yet. I thought I'd wait until we arranged everything, especially now that he's focusing on Carly's situation."

"I won't say a thing," Peter promised. "And as far as your first request, I'll get on the phone and have an officer waiting for you at their office with a warrant. You won't have any problem getting the information you need when you get there. I'll be at a budget meeting for the rest of the day, but call me tomorrow and let me know how it all worked out."

Wayne thanked Peter and then ended the call. It would be a few hours until he reached his destination and he stretched his neck, releasing the tension that had built up over the long night and early start to his day.

As he drove he focused on the winding highway that stretched out ahead of him and the trucks that were merging onto the road, and he didn't notice the faded headlights that had been following him since he pulled away from Bruce Grey's farm.

32

The highway was the same stretch of road that Wayne traveled down countless times before, yet this time it seemed longer than he had remembered.

August normally boasted the deep greens of the forest that lined the highway and the vivid blue that stretched across the sky. This year, however, leaves were turning varying shades of yellow with tinges of orange and red dotting the birch trees leaving the evergreens to stand alone and a gray shroud draped down above him. The coolness was lasting longer each day and evenings were bringing cover of light frost on car windshields in the morning.

Eager gardeners were stretching thin bedsheets over their summering plants that they weren't ready to relinquish to the colder, darker months. While other neighbors gave up the fight.

Wayne had kept his home in Lake Pines, choosing not to sell it when he left for Toronto, and now facing the prospect of returning, he was glad he did. The four-bedroom home had been where he and Josh grew up. Their tree fort still stood in the backyard, the large elm tree forming its trunk around the wood base as it grew to eventually tower over their home. He and Josh spent countless hours in the fort, plotting the epic voyage they wanted to take around the world and the restaurant they'd open when they returned.

Wayne had even proposed a name—The Late Night Eagle. Josh adopted it immediately and they scouted potential locations near the waterfront. It was in the tree fort where the two brothers shared their dreams, hopes, and secrets. It was their refuge and a place where they shared their youth and he could never give it up.

The screen on his phone lit up with a calendar reminder of his niece's birthday. The lock screen image was of him and Lucia, taken a month ago while having dinner with Josh and his husband on Canada Day. An overwhelming swell of love for Lucia threatened to burst through his chest. The time he spent with her made his initial move to Toronto worth everything he left behind. Besides growing the bond with his niece, his relationship with his brother grew stronger.

Josh had not only grown into a smart and reliable police officer, but his job as a parent was what made Wayne the proudest.

Waiting to let Simon know about his decision was one thing, but he felt he owed it to Josh to let him know what he was thinking of doing. Even before he officially resigned.

He brushed his fingers across his screen and opened up his contact app. With one tap, his phone dialed Josh's number.

Giggles and laughs filled the line as Josh screamed into the phone.

"This better be good!"

"Calling to wish my niece a happy birthday should qualify," Wayne joked.

"Hang on," Josh pulled the phone away from his face and called for Lucia. "Uncle Wayne's on the phone!"

A squeal of delight preceded the rustling sound of Lucia wrestling the phone away from Josh's hand.

"Uncle Wayne, are you coming back for my party?" Lucia asked, her tone full of hope. "Daddy is filling the backyard with purple balloons."

Daddy was Josh, and Dad was Thomas. It was clear and simple, but somehow adults became the most confused, where Lucia's friends adjusted and an issue never arose.

"Purple is your favorite color," Wayne exclaimed, pretending to act surprised at the coincidence.

"I know!" exclaimed Lucia.

Wayne spent the next twenty minutes listening to his niece's excitement as she explained every decoration in every corner, along with the games and food that were being prepared for the party. Then, just as eagerly as Lucia dove for the phone, she ended the call.

"I have to go, Dad needs me to help him with the decorations."

Wayne smiled as the call ended, knowing that even though Josh could handle the worst criminals in the city, a room full of eight-year-olds would push him to the brink.

Without thinking, Wayne pressed Simon's number and waited for the call to connect. Poor cellular connection combined with a weakened battery after his extended call with Lucia, caused Simon's voice to fade in and out as he answered the call.

Eventually, the call cut out and the connection was lost. Wayne plugged the phone into the charger and tried the call again. He leaned back in his seat as the phone connected to the car's speaker and Simon's number rang. Much of the traffic had veered south, departing on the off-ramp that took travelers away from Lake Pines along the main highway and Wayne regained the view of the open road ahead. The highway twisted around mounds of Canadian Shield and he caught sporadic views of the lake as he made his way east.

That's when Wayne spotted the truck behind him, inching up on his bumper. Wayne became used to impatient drivers and he slowed down as he drifted onto the paved shoulder. He motioned with his arm from inside the car for the driver to pass and soon the truck was driving around him, but paused briefly, slowing to match Wayne's speed.

Wayne looked to his left as the truck's passenger side window lowered and then an arm stretched toward him.

The next thing Wayne heard was the sound of Simon's voice answering the call and the glass as it shattered next to his face—then everything went dark.

33

Simon pulled the phone away from his face and pressed Wayne's number. This time the phone rang, and instead of a static greeting, his call went to voicemail. Simon left a message and then lowered his phone.

"Sorry about that," Simon apologized to Salma York, the lawyer hired to help clear Carly's name and get her released on bail. "I thought that might be work."

"Do you want me to let you get that?" Salma asked. "I can fill you in later on what happened."

Simon shook his head. This was too important to let it wait.

"No, if you don't mind, I'd like to find out how we can get Carly home."

Salma York, although in her mid-thirties, had already made a name for herself as a litigator. She was calm and focused while being able to maintain a modicum of compassion. She dressed simply, wearing black dress pants and a light beige knit sweater. Her midnight black hair was pulled back in a messy bun and her long slim fingers folded into each other as she spoke. Her mannerisms reminded Simon of his fourth-grade music teacher.

Salma folded her hands on the desk and leaned forward. She brushed a random strand of hair from her cheek and tucked it behind her left ear.

"Although there's evidence of an altercation between Carly and Danny, we could verify her alibi of being at the park with the boys during the same window that was established as the time of death," Salma explained. "However, she still won't elaborate about what happened between her and Danny Blythe."

"Will that be a problem?" Simon asked. He knew how it would look from the standpoint of a police officer, but what he wanted to know was how the legal system would view it.

"It could be," Salma said. "If the prosecutor is having difficulty finding the actual killer. They could circle back to Carly as a potential suspect."

Simon nodded, but only slightly.

"But you know that already," Salma said.

"Can you get Carly released on bail?" Simon asked pointedly. "That's what I want to know."

Salma nodded, "I have a slot booked with the judge today, and I'm hoping that he'll see that the witness

statement along with the killer's profile that he'll see that Carly is an unlikely suspect."

Simon leaned his head sideways, "What profile?"

He had recused himself from the investigation, and along with not being involved directly with any step in the case, he also couldn't access any of the files. The last thing he wanted to do was to jeopardize Carly's freedom.

"Officer Holland sent me the report earlier today," Salma pulled a page out of the file and slid it across the table. "The killer had to be at least six feet to strike the victim where he did on his head. And judging by the damage, the killer is also much stronger than your sister."

Simon read the sheet and noticed that Kerry also had requested to be removed as the coroner in the case when she realized they brought in Carly for questioning, but not before she requested the top forensic investigators in the province. One who had an excellent track record in narrowing down the search of a killer, when there was very little evidence to go on.

"It's not much, but it should be enough to bring up the question of reasonable doubt," Salma explained. "But you and I both know the absolute best way to pull the suspicion away from Carly is to find the killer."

That had been the very conclusion that Simon and Wayne came to the night before.

"And Simon," Salma said, stopping Simon as he was about to walk out the door. "Let Carly know she can trust me. Whatever secret she's holding in could hurt any chance of a solid defense. And at the very least, I can give her some good advice on how to move forward."

"I'll do that. Thanks again Salma."

Simon weighed Carly's options and knew she had few. Carly not only was keeping her secret from her lawyer, Kenny still was in the dark at what Danny Blythe had been bribing her about. Carly was doubly worried because Danny had claimed to have told an associate about what she had done, and she feared another person may still approach her.

Simon was confident that Salma could secure bail for her and his first call was to Kenny who he knew was on his way to see Carly.

His voice was raspy and the wind echoed as he stood on the front steps of the jail speaking with Simon.

"Do you think she can come home today?" Kenny asked.

"That'll be up to the judge, but Salma is going to try her best," Simon explained, trying to sound as hopeful as he could. “I told Salma to call you first once she knows, so keep your phone on.”

Kenny left the chilly steps and ran inside as he ended the call with Simon and promised to stay positive.

Simon called Kerry and thanked her for stepping aside and for posting a top investigator on Carly’s case. She was on her way to meet with someone regarding another case and promised to be next to her phone for any updates.

Simon considered the awkwardness that awaited him in the office and wondered how he’d approach Lukas when he walked through the door. This was, far and away, the most difficult situation he had encountered since he began working in the department.

He didn’t want to deal with any of this, actually. What he wanted to do was drop his boat in the water and disappear for a few hours.

Fishing for the afternoon with Wayne is what lept to his mind.

Simon pulled his phone out of his pocket and tried Wayne’s number, only to have it go to voicemail again. He shoved the phone and his chilled hands into his coat pockets and rushed his steps the last block to the department.

He bounded through the door and then felt everyone’s eyes turn to him.

Sally's face was flush, and a deafening silence washed through the room. Keeping his eyes focused on the crowd of officers in the center of the lobby, Simon turned his head in Sally's direction.

There couldn't be news already about Carly, and if there was, Salma or Kenny would've called him directly, not tracked him down through the department and the officers he worked with.

"Does someone want to tell me what's going on?" Simon asked. The crowd of blank faces stared back at him, no one was able to speak.

The words came from Sally, and even though the room was silent enough for Simon to hear them, he asked her to repeat what she said. Believing that she had made a terrible mistake. But as she repeated the three words, Simon collapsed, unable to deal with hearing it a second time and wanting to scream them away.

34

An emergency crew was dispatched to the highway, where the accident occurred. A truck driver, traveling in the opposite direction, saw Wayne's car as he veered off the main lane on the highway, hit the shoulder, and then lost control. An explosion followed the thundering crunch of metal just as the trucker pulled to the side of the road.

His instinct was to pull Wayne from the car and drag him away from the flames that were crawling up the rocky cliff that the highway carved through and was threatening to engulf the entire vehicle.

It wasn't until they had both fallen to the ground that the truck driver saw the wound to the side of Wayne's head, and realized what caused Wayne to lose control.

The emergency crews arrived without sirens. There was no need. The paramedics found the truck driver, distraught at the side of the road, and had already draped his coat over Wayne's face.

He became even more upset when he learned Wayne was a police officer with the Lake Pines Police Department. The paramedics treated the truck driver for shock and the police took a statement from him. Although, he only remembered seeing Wayne's car collide with the rock at the side of the highway just as a blue GMC truck drove past. Unable to identify the driver or remember a license plate, the driver was free to leave.

The reality of the accident also brought the unbearable weight of the investigation that would follow. Not into Wayne's death, but his murder.

Simon dragged his hand across his face, wiping the tears from his eyes, but they didn't stop flowing.

"I need to call Kerry," Simon blurted out, knowing he would not only want to tell her because Wayne was a friend, but because she'd be the coroner to examine him.

"I'll take care of that," Sally was already lifting the phone to her ear as she dialed Kerry's number.

Simon didn't argue. He didn't want to think about Wayne being gone, let alone say it out loud. But he knew that he'd have to exactly that when it came time to call Josh, and a rush of sadness washed over him.

Moments later, Simon cleared his throat and then spoke to the officers, who were staring down at him. They needed guidance, they needed to know what to do.

Wayne was their boss at one time, not too long ago, and they needed comfort as well as direction. The idea of one of their own being gunned down set the team in motion to find his killer.

A team was assembled and duties were dispersed.

“We need to work as a tight team on this,” Simon explained. “I’ll find out more from the crime scene investigators and then we’ll put a plan in place. For now, I want to find out everything Wayne was working on since he arrived in Lake Pines.”

He turned to face Lukas, “Pull up all the files from Wayne’s computer and forward them to me. There’s a reason he was targeted on the highway and the answer could be in those files. Wayne was no stranger to riling feathers, and he may have poked a little too close to a fire.”

“The files all have to do with the task force he was working on," Lukas said. What he didn’t say, and what he meant, was that the information was under the control and domain of that task force.

“I’ll deal with the jurisdictional issue,” Simon assured Lukas. “I’ll call Peter and make sure no one gets in our way on this.”

Simon left the officers to return to their duties and he made his way to his office. After the door was closed, he picked up his phone.

He took one long, deep breath in and released it as tears filled his eyes. Josh answered on the third ring with a clamoring of children's laughter behind him and the popping of balloons in the background. The sound of a door closing brought the silence Simon needed for what he had to say. After several tries, and with as much composure as he could manage, Simon broke the news to Josh.

35

Kerry rested her hand on Simon's arm as they waited for Josh's plane to land. Neither knew what to say to each other and both welcomed the silence. It was Lucia's laugh that twisted their faces toward the escalator just as the stillness was becoming awkward and painful.

The small girl, with midnight dark eyes, and tight black curls bounced up and down as she held Josh's hand. Both Josh and Thomas were staring at their daughter, hoping that her excitement at being on a plane would help override the sadness that was welling up inside of them.

When the trio reached the bottom of the escalator, Josh fell into Simon's arms while Kerry and Thomas were left with awkward self-introductions in the face of their combined mourning. Kerry had never met Josh or his family, and Simon hadn't seen Josh since he left for Toronto many years earlier.

"Lucia doesn't remember being on a plane," Josh rested his hand on his daughter's head, explaining away her excitement, which seemed misplaced among the adult's tears. "She was just a few months old when we brought her home."

"Daddy, when are we going to see the baby?" Lucia tugged at Josh's arm.

"Soon," Josh smiled at his daughter and then at Kerry. "I wanted her to focus on something happy, so I told her about Dominique."

Kerry crouched down, so her face was next to Lucia's, "Dominique will be so excited to meet you."

Lucia smiled and hugged her stuffed bear with her left arm as she leaned her head against Josh's body.

Thomas and Kerry took Lucia to the baggage carousel and waited for their suitcases to be unloaded from the airplane, leaving Simon and Josh alone.

"I had just spoken with him minutes before," Josh's words stopped there. He still was unable to mention Wayne's death without crying.

He and Simon had spent over an hour on the phone the evening before. Their shock at Wayne's death was primarily what they talked about. Fate had played a hand in Wayne calling to wish Lucia a happy birthday, and it was something Josh couldn't ignore. Simon had wondered what his missed calls with Wayne indicated, and he struggled to find meaning in the last moments of their time together.

"Are you any closer to finding out who's responsible for this?" Josh asked.

"Everything happened so quickly, and since that stretch of the highway was so remote, there was only the one witness."

"The truck driver who stopped?" Josh asked. "What about the blue truck he saw pass Wayne just before his car went off the road?"

"We have a few leads, but we still haven't been able to find it or the driver."

"Do you have any idea where he was going?" Josh asked as he glanced over at Lucia who was jumping up and down after she spotted her bubblegum pink suitcase tumbling down the shoot. "That stretch of highway is at least half an hour east of Lake Pines."

"Officer Holland was working closely with him the last few days. I'm having him go through Wayne's files now and hopefully, we'll have some idea by the time we get back to Lake Pines."

"I want to help," Josh's words were not just the statement of a bereaved brother, but those of a police officer who knew he had something of value to offer to the investigation.

"I'm going to speak with the five survivors this afternoon," Simon said. "We've convinced them to move to a hotel for their own safety. They weren't too keen on being held longer than necessary, but once we told them what happened to Wayne, they agreed."

Thomas and Lucia had pulled their suitcases from the carousel and were walking toward the door with Kerry. Simon put his hand on Josh's shoulder and they followed them as they headed to the parking garage where Simon had parked. The two-hour drive was filled mostly with silence as everyone contemplated how they were going to deal with the difficult days ahead of them. Lucia, however, was contemplating how she was going to keep her bear from falling asleep. After dropping Thomas and Lucia at Wayne's house, Simon and Josh drove directly to the hotel where the five survivors were waiting.

"Do you want me to drop you off at home?" Simon asked Kerry as he and Josh climbed back into his truck.

"No, I still have some work to do on an old case," Kerry said, lying and wondering how she was going to get out to Airplane Island and then back before dark. "I'll just see you at home later."

Simon and Josh pulled out of the driveway and Kerry watched as they turned left at the end of the street and hoped that they had better luck than she had with the John Doe case on Airplane Island.

36

Kerry had been on her way to Airplane Island when Sally called and informed her about Wayne's accident. Her reaction of shock was quickly followed by anger. A tightness clawed at her stomach, the pain and sadness too much to hold in and Kerry pulled over to the side of the road and cried.

Her use of Wayne's log-in credentials was the first thing to jump to mind when she heard of his murder. Kerry nervously wondered if his death had something to do with her work for Agent Miller, and anger and fear pulsed through her veins. Kerry wanted to make everything stop, she had never wanted to be wrapped up in a secret murder investigation, and she was even willing to walk away from the information that was promised to her.

Her anger was even more pronounced since Wayne's death and she wanted to lash out at someone but wasn't sure in which direction to strike. The only thing she could focus on was her work, and the autopsy she had completed on Wayne was the most difficult examination she conducted. It took her longer to complete the autopsy, having to leave the lab between her bouts of tears. And that too brought her anger.

The overwhelming feeling of having her hands tied gave her no outlet to express her frustration. It reminded her of when she was in her final year of university and a professor, who for some unknown reason, had taken a dislike to her, had given her a failing grade on her final paper. The professor also was on the university panel that oversaw all complaints lodged with the dean and his longstanding record as a popular faculty member made it difficult to have anyone believe Kerry's accusation that she was unfairly targeted and falsely graded.

Her best friend had given her some advice, which at the time seemed odd, 'fight him at his own game'. Kerry remembered those words of advice as she drove out to Airplane Island.

Neither of the agents was expecting her, and she knew that the information about who John Doe was had to be somewhere on that island. Finding out who he was and what the secret was behind him, would at least confirm if it was the reason Wayne was killed. And if Wayne's death could be connected to what she had helped the two agents do, then Kerry would make them pay.

She had never given the small microchip she found embedded in John Doe's arm. Something about Agent Miller's extreme secretiveness prompted Kerry to hang onto it for insurance. Even though there was no way for her to find out what was on the small computer chip, Agent Miller would be able to.

Kerry pulled away from the small dock and took a widened path around the islands as she approached Airplane Island. She cut the engine and drifted the boat, nestling the bow in between a pile of rocks, and out of view of the cottage.

She crawled out of the boat, up the side of the rocky island, and then crouched low as she hid inside the dense brush. It was a few hours until sunset, and a heavy chill had filled the air. The island was quiet, as Kerry strained her ears to listen for the sound of steps or people talking. She heard neither.

She could see the tip of the chimney from the edge of the bushes she was hiding behind, and a small trail of smoke curled up from the faded rock stack. Out of the corner of her eye, Kerry saw an angled cellar door built into the ground. The wooden door, painted a deep green, sat twenty feet from the back of the canvas tent.

Kerry lifted the door and peered inside. A faint light from a single bulb glowed at the bottom of a set of steps. She closed the door as she walked down the steps and turned the corner. Inside was a small room, filled with walls layered with pictures of targets, and names of people that Agent Miller and Agent Davis held 'of interest'. John Doe sat in the middle of the pages with his actual name and his official rank typed underneath.

Alongside his image were lines drawn to the names of several government officials and two corporations. Kerry leaned forward to get a close look at the names as the room lit up. She turned around to see the two agents were standing behind her.

37

Simon arrived at the Lakeside Motel just as lunch was being arranged on a long table in a private dining area. It was a simple setup, but one where both the survivors and their families could be together. The last thing anyone wanted was for any of the individuals who had suffered such a horrific experience to feel like they were prisoners again.

Simon gathered everyone in the room and closed the doors. He tried to soften the news of Wayne's death, but as he put his elbows on the table and leaned forward, the seriousness of Wayne's murder was clear. He introduced Josh, and awkward glances passed between everyone in the room. The idea of moving forward without Wayne, who they had learned to trust was difficult enough, now they were asked to trust a complete stranger. Even if the man standing in front of them was Wayne's brother, he was still, nevertheless a stranger.

The five shared looks of unease between themselves, and their concern and fear were difficult to hide. Questions passed between them with just a side glance or a blink. These five were not just scared, they were terrified.

It was Russ who spoke first, and Simon thought, the unofficial spokesperson for the group, "How do we know we'll be safe? If they could get to Officer Burgess, then they can get to us too."

"You're right," Simon said, shocking both the group of survivors and the few family members standing with them. "But you're free and at least have a chance, and we'll do whatever is in our power to protect you. But there are so many other people we still need to save and a big part of that is also stopping the two men who kidnapped you and held you captive."

Silence and nervous fidgeting filled the small room. It was Callie who spoke first. Simon remembered the stars that Wayne marked next to Callie's name in his file. She, he had determined, was the connection he had to make if he was going to break through to the rest of the group. Callie had a street toughness that Wayne recognized and he knew she would be the key to their success.

And he was right.

Callie stepped forward, pushing her fears aside and looking only to herself for strength, and told Simon the name of the contact she knew was helping arrange their move out of Lake Pines.

38

Lukas was writing on the second whiteboard in the office, listing the contacts Wayne made over the last forty-eight hours. Nothing was out of the ordinary or deviated from the plan that he had told Lukas they were going to follow. Tracking down the kidnappers had to be systematic and procedures were to be strictly followed.

"That wasn't always how Wayne did things," Simon recalled as the three officers tried to make sense of the pattern Wayne followed shortly before his death.

"And Wayne didn't tell you where he was going the morning he was killed?" Josh asked.

"No," Lukas answered, shaking his head. "We were supposed to meet in the morning and go over the survivors' testimony before they were going to be released from the hospital. Wayne knew we couldn't keep them there any longer and he was afraid that if we let them go, that we may never find out what really happened, or who the kidnappers were."

"So why, if it was so important to Wayne to keep the survivors in the hospital, would he leave town without taking one last attempt to speak with them?" Simon asked them.

Lukas shrugged his shoulders and Josh shifted his body against the wall. Neither of them had an answer.

"Think, guys," Simon slammed his hand against the wall. "We all know that Wayne would've believed that one of those survivors had information otherwise he wouldn't have risked his badge to illegally try and hold them against their will."

"As it turned out, he was right," Josh said referring to the name Callie gave them earlier.

A cold feeling tightened around Simon's body, "When he left our place, he never said anything about a break in the case. Things like that Wayne could never push aside, he lived and breathed his work. I saw him the night before he died and he never gave me any indication that he was close to something big on the case."

"That must mean that some point after he left your place and the time he was killed, that he stumbled across some evidence that prompted him to leave town," Josh guessed. "He must have been following a lead."

Lukas dropped into the chair in front of Wayne's computer and pulled up the history log from the day before Wayne died. He scrolled past the searches and files they both worked on until Lukas left at five, and then noticed the three files that Wayne had opened last, and then printed.

"Why was Wayne searching through Carly's file?" Josh asked.

Simon's throat tightened and he felt a warmth rise to his face.

What if Wayne's murder had nothing to do with the kidnappers and it had everything to do with the secret that brought Danny Blythe back into their lives.

Lukas handed the printouts to Josh who laid them on the table and the three men looked at them and tried to figure out what it was that Wayne saw.

Simon was focused on the mugshot image of Danny Blythe unable to move his eyes away from his face and Josh was trying to figure out what the invoice related to. But it was Lukas who spotted the connection and when he told them about the testimony given by Bruce Grey and then pointed to the invoice found in Danny Blythe's trailer, they saw it too.

The pieces were beginning to click into place, like a distorted puzzle, and Simon could see why Wayne didn't tell Lukas what he found. Wayne was trying to protect Carly until he confirmed his suspicions and he had left himself open and vulnerable.

Lukas took two other officers and headed directly to Bruce Grey's farm. They arrived back at the station with the disgruntled and obstinate old man who had even less interest in cooperating than he did the first time he was arrested.

Any sympathy, what little there was, for Bruce Grey had evaporated once Simon realized that Wayne had visited him just before he died. He didn't care how long the old man was left to wait and wonder why he was dragged back into the station for further questioning. However, he was eager to find Wayne's killer and hopefully stop the transport by the human traffickers before it was too late.

He owed it to Wayne to finish what his friend had started, he didn't want Wayne's death to be in vain.

Bruce Grey struggled against his slouching shoulders, heavy with age, and forced his body straight. His head wobbled slightly on his thin neck and a stale odor of tobacco and rye filled the small room.

Wayne slammed a file on the table as he and Josh sat down across from him.

The old man's lip quivered as the two officers glared at him. He knew this was about more than renting the barn to the kidnappers and it was definitely about more than his evading taxes on the side businesses and deals he had made over the years.

Bruce Grey had a rough life, and during the moments in his life where he was young and more agile, he ran with a tougher crowd. People who wouldn't think twice to exact revenge if they felt someone they cared about had been hurt. The type of men who wasted no time worrying about repercussions or allotting any space in their hearts for guilt.

When revenge was necessary, they just simply took care of business.

The two men sitting across the table from him had the same look in their eyes as they stared down at him. The fact that they were both cops, Bruce knew, wouldn't factor into the equation.

What had begun as a serious police investigation had turned personal, and Bruce Grey was in the path of the two men he now faced as they searched for answers.

39

"I want a lawyer," Bruce Grey announced seconds after Simon and Josh sat across from him.

When he mentioned he didn't have one, Simon arranged to have a court-appointed lawyer brought in. Segal Prince arrived twenty minutes later, tucking his shirt into his waistband and insisting he have some time to confer with his client.

"Your client has information that directly pertains to kidnapped victims that are in danger of being transferred out of the country by human traffickers," Simon explained. "By all means protect his rights, but we need to find out where these kids are so we can save them."

Simon left out the fact that one of the kidnappers is also suspected of having killed a police officer and instead focused on the one issue that he would have trouble arguing in court.

“Mr. Grey has information that if held back, will be the equivalent of destroying evidence,” Simon said. “And that makes our questions extremely time-sensitive.”

Segal spoke with Bruce Grey and after the promise of cooperation and possible leniency, the old man agreed to answer their questions.

Benji Jones and Alex Johnson. Those were the two names that Wayne had been searching for since he first spoke with Chloe Stuart after she managed to escape from the barn on Bruce Grey’s property.

And one of them was connected to Danny Blythe, but when pressed for an answer, Bruce Grey claimed to not know which one.

They had arrived with Danny when they wanted to arrange to lease a section of Bruce Grey’s property.

“Alex, I think he was the leader, said that they’d need it for two years at least,” the old man explained. “Paid me cash upfront for the use of the barn and to keep from renting the back lot out to farmers.”

“Why didn’t you tell Officer Burgess that?” Simon asked. “He could’ve tracked them down sooner.”

“Not likely,” the old man scoffed. “The smaller one, they called him Jay, I don’t think he liked his name. Said it reminded him of a bad television show about a dog.

Anyway, the smaller one, said if they ever were caught that they'd make sure I'd pay."

At that moment, the old man dragged his frail and shaky hand across the front of his neck. No one needed to ask what he was referencing, and the color drained from Segal's face. It was clear this was the closest the lawyer had been to a threat and Simon wondered what cases he had been working on up until the moment he met Bruce Grey.

"They came and went through the night and I never asked any questions," the old man explained. "I knew they were up to something illegal, but I never imagined it was that bad."

The old man's fingers crumpled into a fist and he slammed it against the top of the table. "I have a niece that I'd protect with my life, and there's no way that I would've allowed any of that to go on."

Bruce Grey was one of the least likable individuals that Simon had met, but something in his wobbling voice and strained eyes allowed Simon to believe at least that much about him.

There were lines that even criminals drew, and it was clear where Bruce Grey drew his line.

A knock on the door paused Simon's questions and he and Josh gave the old man an opportunity to confer with his lawyer and wondered how Segal Prince was going to explain that no matter how cooperative he was, that charges were most definitely going to be laid.

Simon doubted that the newly minted lawyer would be able to argue Bruce Grey out of prison, and for a brief moment, he felt sorry for what lay ahead for him. But that too passed.

When Simon and Josh stepped out of the interrogation room, Peter was waiting for them.

"I came as soon as I could," Peter shook both of their hands and then placed a firm hand on Josh's shoulder. "I can't tell you how sorry I am, Josh. Wayne was an amazing person."

Josh, unable to speak, just nodded his head.

"I was out of the office yesterday afternoon and only heard about Wayne's death when I got in this morning," Peter apologized. "Sorry I didn't come sooner."

"You didn't have to come all the way down, but we appreciate it."

"But I did," Peter said. "I knew where he was going when he was killed."

"How?" Josh asked as he looked to Simon and then back to Peter.

"He called me because he needed to ensure he had access to some files in an office, and he didn't think he'd have enough time to get the authorization or a warrant issued from Toronto," Peter explained. "I arranged for a few officers to meet Wayne there with a warrant. When I got into the office this morning, I saw that they left a message. They waited for Wayne and he never showed up. They wanted to know what they should do next."

Simon dragged his fingers through his hair, "No one here knew he was heading anywhere, and I'm sure the other officers on his task force didn't either."

"They were all reassigned," Lukas said.

"Where was he going?" Josh asked.

"I have a helicopter waiting," Peter said. "If we leave now we'll get to the pier before the ship leaves."

"The pier? Where?"

"Thunder Bay."

40

The port of Thunder Bay, located at the head of the Great Lakes and the St. Lawrence Seaway system, made it the ideal waterway to transport a variety of smuggled items.

Drugs, stolen cars, and most recently, it became a hub for human traffickers. International transports move through the area with ease and the access for trucks to move across the country without check stops made it an ideal port. Many criminals were taking advantage of the infrastructure legitimate businesses had established at the port.

Ships with small corners of space were loaded with illegal cargo containers, some filled with drugs and stolen goods, others loaded with human cargo. Although port employees are trained to spot and report illegal activity, all too often employees are willing to take bribes to either look the other way or to adjust manifests for ships to allow illegal cargo to move under the guise and umbrella of unsuspecting legal trade.

Finding the connection and the link to the kidnappers was key in the human trafficking task force capturing human traffickers and rescuing victims.

It was the small piece of ripped paper in the jacket Wayne found in the mine that eventually linked the kidnappers to the port. The specific grease Kerry identified when she tested the spot on the jacket's sleeve pointed to a location outside of Lake Pines. But it was the random piece of paper that Danny Blythe had scribbled a list of items he was preparing to buy that filled in the blanks.

Simon read the file as the helicopter sped the group toward the port where Wayne was headed on the morning he was killed.

"Danny must have grabbed the sheet when he was helping Alex and Benji get established and set up in the barn on Bruce Grey's farm," Simon said. "The type of corner brackets, floor plates, and padlocks that Danny had itemized on this list were the exact ones that were used to construct the holding cells in the barn."

"He must've grabbed the sheet from either Benji or Alex's desk when he was told to get them," Lukas guessed.

"Benji's signature was on the bottom of the invoice, so he was probably the one in charge of getting the shipping containers. It looks like he purchased them a few months before we found the victims in the mine," Josh said. "Which aligns with the time Chloe said a bulk of the victims had started to disappear."

"And she said that they were looking to transport the last few out this week," Simon added and then looked out the window, deep in thought. "There are so many young kids that Wayne saved, yet, there are so many more that slip through the cracks."

"There's something else that's bothering me," Lukas said. "A shipping container is quite large and you and Wayne only rescued five people from that mine."

"They were being hidden there until they could be moved," Simon said. "I guess Chloe escaping moved up their plan. They must have been adding them to another group of kidnapped victims."

Peter shook his head, "It's all so cold."

The others agreed. And they knew that they had to do their best to stop the last shipment of human cargo from leaving."

The helicopter landed on the end of the pier in the designated flight landing area. As Peter had hoped, the police officers and warrants were waiting when they landed. After a brief introduction, the team ran toward the office where the office clerk was caught off guard. She was young, maybe in her late twenties, and even though she was shown and read the warrant, Simon was certain she had no idea what it all meant.

She showed the officers the files containing the shipping manifests and then watched as they fanned through the pages.

"Are there any ships leaving today that had last-minute deliveries?" Josh asked.

The girl nodded and pulled a sheet out of the pile on the corner of her desk and held it out for Josh.

"My boss got a call yesterday that there would be a container delivered to Pier 7," the girl pointed out the window to the far end of the port.

In the distance, lights shone down on the end of the pier and a multitude of shadows hurried around the crane as a truck was backing up close to the ship.

As Peter radioed to the team waiting outside the office on the pier, the group ran out of the office and dashed their way toward Pier 7. Separating and fanning out in different directions, they cut off any access of escape from the pier.

The ship had been loaded with forestry products and the last-minute delivery was listed as a shipping container of wood pellets. However, it was highly unlikely since the truck arriving was coming from an area where Simon knew the lumber mill had been closed.

Peter waved five officers toward the north end of the pier while he worked his way around the south side with Simon, Lukas, and Josh. Leaving the remaining officers to block off the exit from the pier. The water would be the only way for Benji or Alex to escape.

A pier worker who was helping unload the shipping container from the truck bed turned just as a few officers rounded the corner and yelled to the others. Soon workers were scrambling away from the truck, some hiding behind containers or running onto the ship and some sprawled themselves on the ground, surrendering before a fight was necessary.

The frantic dash sent people in every direction and the team that was approaching a strategic group found themselves separated and running after the escapees.

Simon had committed the image of Benji and Alex to memory and realized that soon the man in the red hat he was chasing was Benji Jones.

Light reflected off the metal in Benji's left hand and Simon kept his eye trained on the gun while he continued to chase him. He followed Benji when he veered left, trapping them both in a small aisle that had containers stacked three high on each side, and a wall on the end.

It was a dead-end stop and as Benji turned around to run toward Simon, he was met with Simon's raised arm and a weapon pointing directly at him.

Simon told him not to move and walked slowly as he motioned for Benji to drop his gun.

Benji shook his head, "Not until we reach an agreement." His words were sure but his face and eyes revealed he was terrified.

He knew what he was up against if Simon arrested him and took him in, and he also knew what would happen if he tried to run.

Benji waved his gun in the air, "I can help you catch the big guy. The one in charge."

Simon didn't flinch, "Turn around and drop your gun."

Again, Benji raised his arms and shifted his eyes around the pier, beyond Simon and the officers running toward them. He was frantic to strike a bargain and had offered to turn evidence against Alex and the contact who arranged the sale of the kids they had transported to the pier.

"He also killed someone," Benji blurted out as if he was tossing a life ring for a drowning victim. But the person drowning was him.

Simon stared straight into Benji's face.

“I’m serious,” Benji’s voice wobbled. “And some cop’s sister is taking the heat for it. That has to be worth something?”

Simon’s face froze at the mention of what must have been Danny’s murder.

“You’re bluffing,” Simon snapped. “Turn around and drop the gun.”

“I’m not! I’ll testify to it too,” Benji, eager to prove he was telling the truth went a step further. "Danny was trying to double-cross Alex and get more money out of him. That’s when Alex said Danny was too much of liability especially because he was also trying to shake down a cop and his sister.”

Simon held his gun firm, “About what?”

“A secret he had on her.”

“Can you prove it?” Simon asked.

Benji nodded his head.

Simon pressed his finger against the trigger, the weight of the gun urging him to make a decision.

The echoed steps of the officers running down the pier rebounded off the wall of stacked shipping containers where he had Benji trapped.

It would be only a few seconds before they rounded the last rust-colored container and had a full view of Simon with his gun leveled at Benji’s body. Benji, armed but nowhere to run.

He had to make a decision and it needed to be now.

The alarm was growing louder, and Simon couldn't be sure if the signal was shifting or if he was just focusing on it more. Benji relaxed his shoulders, and then saw the change in Simon's eyes, he lowered his arm and the gun barrel was pointing in Simon's direction.

Josh and Lukas turned the corner, just as the shot exploded.

41

It was the first funeral they had attended since the pandemic restrictions had relaxed. Most of the town had turned out to pay respect to one of their own, who through his act of protecting them, had died.

The Whitecap Pavilion on the lakefront was reserved for Wayne's funeral, and as Simon looked out over the crowd he smiled. He knew Wayne would be looking down and laughing at the standing-room-only crowd, shoved shoulder to shoulder, and joked that they had all showed up by mistake.

But it was no error. Everyone in attendance would brave their fear of being in a crowd and next to so many people as they honored Wayne's memory. Simon knew everyone pushed aside their appointments and work schedules because it was the right thing to do.

It was during funerals that family and friends learned a lot about each other. Many people hadn't been aware that Wayne was a key member of the Human Trafficking Task Force and that he was responsible for saving many young victims. It was the memory of the ones who he didn't save that haunted him. He was a regular volunteer at the Red Cross Blood Bank, and after Dominique was born, Wayne made a donation in her name to the Children's Hospital.

The crowd was filled with neighbors Wayne knew since he was a child. Teachers who once admonished him for his immaturity in their classrooms had grown to respect the man who became a leader in their community. A collection of fishing buddies, friends he played hockey with, and especially the few close friends he considered family.

Oliver, Kerry, Simon, and Dominique sat alongside Josh, Thomas, and Lucia. They were now each other's family, perpetually connected by Wayne. Lucia busied herself adjusting Dominique's hat, looking up she smiled at Kerry and said she was practicing to be an older sister. Kerry looked at Josh who slowly shook his head back and forth while Thomas tried not to laugh.

Carly was sitting a few rows behind with her husband and refused Kerry's offer to sit with the family. Her emotions were stretched to the edges, and Kerry wasn't even sure how much sleep Carly had the night before. Simon was relieved that Carly's lawyer was able to have her released on bail, and although everyone who knew her believed she was innocent, she spent most of the day with her head held down.

The rows directly behind them were reserved for the people Wayne would want to have next to his family. They were filled with the individuals who he had rescued. Some came with family or friends, but all came for the same reason.

Joining the group were the five survivors that were finally free from Benji Jones and Alex Johnson.

Wayne would have joked that the hour-long service was an hour longer than necessary. But when she stood to join the crowd of friends at the back of the tent, she knew he'd be wrong.

Kerry spotted Jenna Bean, who was standing next to her mother, their arms wrapped around each other while they spoke with Russ and Callie at the back of the tent. Away from the crowd.

"I hope I'm not interrupting," Kerry said as she walked up beside them. Dominique had fallen asleep and rested her head on Kerry's shoulder.

Jenna reached up and stroked the back of Dominique's head, "She's so cute!"

Everyone, Russ included, couldn't help but gush over the sleeping child in Kerry's arms.

Kerry was overcome with emotion as she stood next to Jenna and Russ. They were children themselves. Kerry told them how brave they were, and how proud she was of them for coming forward in the end.

"It was hard, but we owed our lives to Wayne," Jenna said. "I was just so terrified of what might happen if we did."

"But not everyone was so lucky," Russ said, and Jenna seemed to lean close to his body as they remembered the pain they shared.

Jenna's eyes widened, "But some did escape. Especially a few girls who were there before us. I think one of them was pregnant when she got away."

"That's right," Russ said. "I remember hanging onto that story and hoping it would be me one day."

"Amy knew her," Callie tapped a finger to her chin and she closed her eyes, deep in thought. "What was her name?"

"Was it Katie?" Russ spoke up, remembering the same story.

"That's it!" Callie slapped her hand on Russ's shoulder. "Katie."

"Unfortunately, she wasn't the only one who found themselves with a baby," Russ said, in a low voice. "That's why some of the kids were kidnapped in the first place, to have babies."

Kerry had heard about the underground baby mills and instinctively pulled Dominique close to her chest.

"But that's not what happened with her," Callie said.

Kerry listened and as Callie spoke she realized something they missed in the timeline. Either that, or one of the five survivors wasn't telling the truth. Kerry excused herself from the group and found Simon in the middle of a conversation with Mrs. Marsh.

Kerry tugged Simon's elbow, pulling him away from the group he was speaking with. She stood out of view of the crowd and made sure she was far away from where anyone could hear. Especially out of earshot of the one person she needed to tell Simon about.

42

Alex Johnson was led in cuffs to the small interrogation room at the end of the hall. He was treated with more respect than any of the guards deemed acceptable, so they intentionally made every step as awkward and painful as they could, as they rushed him down the hall.

Alex's complaints and protests and the guard's hurried steps were ignored, and he knew that even if he mentioned it to his lawyer, that he would only suggest that Alex keep quiet if he wanted to find any chance of leniency.

At thirty-eight, Alex Johnson was climbing the ladder faster than he had expected and was inching his way closer to the main operation in Duluth. He had proven himself loyal, both on the streets and during his nine-month stint in prison when he was eighteen. No matter how he was pressured by the prosecutor, or even by his own lawyer, he never flinched when he was on the stand. Even though he wasn't the one holding the gun when the shopkeeper fell, he refused to reveal who it was that had been in charge of the gang that was working the Danforth area in Toronto.

He was rewarded handsomely for his silence, and as a result, had been given his own territory where he controlled the distribution of drugs. From there, it was only a few years before Max approached him and suggested another move. This time, his operation would have an international affiliation.

Alex hadn't planned to be part of an operation that would lure and then siphon kids off to human traffickers. In fact, he hated the idea. But unlike prison, there was no one on the street offering him a way out or an opportunity to trade someone else's freedom for his own. He was a lifer with no way out.

Except for the one time that Danny Blythe had approached him and tried to blackmail him, Alex had established an untouchable persona that kept him safe from being caught. Until the night he was on Pier 7.

He was angry with himself for not getting rid of Chloe Stuart earlier. She had resisted from the first day she was brought in. Her unwillingness to cooperate with Alex was what placed her in the situation where she was then going to be sent overseas. Two shipments were being closed out by the end of the month. One had already left for the west coast and the last one was heading to Europe, in a container and on a ship that was leaving Thunder Bay.

Chloe was supposed to be on that ship. Her escape and contact with the police is what prompted the rushed move out of Bruce Grey's barn, and left them open to leave a trail.

It was also when Danny Blythe reappeared. He was initially referred by Benji, who Alex reluctantly took on as an associate. Although Benji didn't seem capable of making too many decisions on his own, Alex believed his lack of intelligence may actually make him more malleable in the field. Up until the moment he introduced Danny Blythe, he had been a quiet and cooperative member of the operation. But Danny wanted in - he wanted to be part of the bigger operation, and he was pressuring Benji to recommend him to Alex.

It was too late by the time Alex realized Danny knew too much. When he first arrived in Lake Pines, he had used him to secure the farm and even to purchase the supplies necessary to set up the cells. However, having two dimwitted and unreliable underlings to control was not what Alex wanted to do. So he dismissed Danny and put off making a decision hoping he'd go away.

Instead, Danny returned with a bribe in mind and threatened to reveal their operation and location. In between hiding and planning his escape through the port in Thunder Bay, he took care of Danny and thought that he had heard the last of it.

Now, as he was pushed down into the hard plastic chair, and his cuffs secured to a hook on the side of the desk, Alex wondered if his luck had run out.

A tall police officer walked into the room with a second close behind. He didn't recognize either of them, but he knew it was the taller one who had cornered Benji. Alex almost wanted to thank him, the cop had no idea what a favor he had done for him. Benji would've turned on Alex in an instant if it meant his own freedom.

Unlike Alex, Benji hadn't learned his loyalty on the streets and he didn't have the years invested in staying alive. The scars Alex both received and gave were proof of that. The cops weren't friendly as they introduced themselves, nor were they forthcoming on why they wanted to speak with him.

"Alex," Simon said as he leaned into the back of his seat. "Have you reconsidered our offer?"

Alex folded his hands together and lowered them to his lap. Each finger, along with the backside of his hands were covered with an assortment of tattoos. Markings stretched up each arm and along the left side of his neck. From reading his file, Simon also knew that his back had the markings for a gang that normally worked the west coast and had rumored clashes with several police districts stretching from north of Bella Coola, British Columbia stopping just shy of Sacramento, California. For all intents and purposes, Alex Johnson grew up in a gang family.

Simon asked him again. Alex's continued silence was his answer.

The file sat closed on the table between them. Simon tapped the top of the file, "We've received a transfer request for you."

Alex smiled, he hoped it was the Kamloops Correctional Facility. He still had connections there, and it at least would make the time he would have to be inside a little easier.

"You don't have anything," Alex goaded Simon as the second cop sat silently beside him. "Otherwise you wouldn't be here."

"The five survivors have all identified you and Benji," Simon said. "And there was a general consensus that you were in charge."

Alex grinned, his thin lips stretched across his face, revealing a hideous laugh, "How do you not know it wasn't the other way around?"

Simon was prepared for him to say that and knew the only way to get the upper hand was to throw out a random ball, hoping to set him off balance.

Simon returned the grin, "I guess I don't. But then again, maybe the American authorities can figure it out."

Simon pushed his chair back and stood just as a wash of panic crossed over Alex's face.

"What do you mean the Americans?" Alex knew enough to know that if he ended up south of the border, that there was no protection for him. He tugged at the chains, shaking the table, but not moving it from its base. "You can't do that!"

"We can - if we think that we don't have anything strong enough to hold you on here," Simon lied. "And the U.S. authorities are pretty confident that they have enough on your involvement and connection with the human traffickers in Duluth."

Alex grew nervous and fidgeted in his seat and grew more frustrated with the lack of movement because of the chains.

"We also have your truck," Simon said. "You stupidly drove it to Thunder Bay basically giving us the evidence we need to pin two murders on you."

The blue GMC truck that was identified as having passed Wayne just before he was shot also had a broken and bloodied baseball bat thrown on the floor behind the driver's seat.

Sensing his own defeat, Alex agreed to give Simon some information about how he coordinated the kidnapping of the kids and then brought them to the human traffickers, but refused to give up the name of his boss. He, Alex said, would find no forgiveness in his betrayal.

Simon listened while Alex explained the process he and a few others took in luring kids off the street and into a position where they were drugged and then abducted. He spoke like he was giving a recipe for a casserole. No feeling, emotion, or regret. It was everything Simon could do, not to jump across the table at Alex Johnson.

"We used a girl to lure the kids because she was easier to trust than we were."

Simon scanned over Alex's scarred and tattooed face and had no trouble seeing why.

"Once she secured their trust, we got some kids started on selling drugs, and the ones that were more valuable we passed along to the traffickers."

Simon had to steady himself from not becoming ill.

"Can you give us the name of the girl who worked with you on the streets?"

Alex nodded, his evil grin stretched as he released the name. Without a word, Simon stood and left the room.

43

Kerry placed the photograph of Katie Lancaster on the table and positioned it to be in direct line with Amy Hanover's eyes. Amy looked at the photo, barely blinking, and then lifted her face to meet Kerry's.

"Do you recognize this girl?" Kerry wanted to lunge across the table and shake the answer out of Amy.

Katie's resemblance to Dominique was striking. The soft curls that naturally fell around the side of Katie's face and the small dimple that etched her left cheek, mirrored Dominique's. Her eyes were hopeful and happy and Kerry saw in the picture the reflection of a girl who, at one point in her life, was filled with optimism.

Amy leaned forward and unlike Chloe, Russ, Callie, or Jenna, she didn't move to touch the picture. The others were drawn to Katie's picture with the knowledge that they had experienced the same trauma. Although it was at a different time, the nightmare they shared made them part of the same world. They were part of a club they had no desire to be a part of but had been marked for the rest of their lives because of the experience. But none of them recognized Katie.

Some of the survivors would rebound quicker than others, and a few would go on to build lives around saving future victims from the same fate. Whatever the draw, the connection was permanent.

When Chloe held the picture, she ran her finger over Katie's image and tried to imagine the young girl as if she were sitting next to her. Russ, Callie, and Jenna all formed tears when they learned Katie was like them. That she was one of them. They each used different words to express their inquisitiveness but they all wanted to know who she was and how she escaped.

Amy did neither.

"I guess she looks kinda familiar," Amy squirmed in her seat. It would have been a move that would've been missed if Kerry wasn't looking for it.

"She was one of Alex Johnson's victims," Kerry said. "I was wondering what you knew about her?"

Amy shrugged her shoulders, "We just all tried to mind our own business and keep to ourselves, so I wouldn't know." She pushed her hands down on her lap and her eyes darted to the door. "Is that all?"

Kerry ignored Amy's question, "I'm a bit confused."

"About?" Amy asked.

"You told Officer Burgess that you'd been held by Alex and Benji for ten months."

"That's right," Amy's neck began to rise to dark pink.

"But you told Callie about a girl who was there before her that became pregnant and died."

"Maybe I was just trying to scare her," Amy snapped. "It was pretty scary in there."

"I'm sure it was," Kerry said. "For the ones who were actually held against their will."

Amy looked at Simon who was leaning against the wall and then darted her eyes toward Kerry. Her jaw dropped open, shock and dismay covered her face and tainted her voice, "What are you implying?"

"How did you know Katie was pregnant?"

Amy grabbed the edge of the table with her hand, gripping it so tightly that her knuckles turned white.

"You would only know that she was pregnant if you were there at the same time she was."

Amy was growing nervous, and Kerry could see her chest rise and fall with each tense breath.

Kerry let her hand fall next to Katie's picture, resting it like a mother would when protecting her child.

"And you would only know she died if you were part of it."

Amy noticed Simon move and she pushed her chair back and stumbled to her feet.

Kerry stood, grabbed Katie's picture, and held it up, "Katie died, but her daughter survived, and I think you know what happened. Help us give Katie some justice, so her daughter can have some peace."

Simon pulled his handcuffs from the back of his waistband and reached out for Amy's arm.

"Wait!" Amy shouted. "Maybe we can make a deal or something?"

"It depends on what you have," Simon said, speaking for the first time.

Amy looked down, her fingers nervously picked at the edge of her nails. She began to cry, tears rolled down her cheek and she briskly wiped them away.

The words she was about to say rolled around in her mind, as she tried to decide what to say and what would help her situation.

"It was an accident," Amy said. "Alex sent me out to find her. He gave me his truck and told me not to come back without her. I saw her walking along the road and I pulled over and tried to convince her to get into the truck with me. I told her that I'd drive her to the bus station."

"You lied. Just like you did when you helped Benji and Alex lure kids into being abducted."

Amy looked away, her eyes filled with tears, "How do you think I ended up there? Cooperating with Alex was the only way to stay alive. I hated doing it, but I was too afraid of what would happen if I didn't."

Kerry and Simon sat silently as Amy tried to calm her breathes. She wiped her face with the sleeve of her shirt and then sat back down in the chair.

"I tried to get Katie to get into the truck but she wouldn't trust me and she took off. I knew if I came back without her that Alex would kill me, so I drove after her," Amy folded her hand over her face and screamed, her words full of tears. "It happened so fast, I never meant to hit her!"

The words were like a punch to Kerry's gut. She knew that Katie had died the night that Dominique was born, it was something she learned when she spoke with Gloria. Kerry imagined feeling relief at knowing who had hit her that night, and she thought she'd feel relieved at bringing that person to justice.

Instead, Kerry felt pain and despair. When she looked into the eyes of Katie's killer she wanted to feel hate but the only emotion that came was sadness. Because no matter how hard she tried she could only see Amy Hanover as another one of Alex Johnson's victims.

44

Serena Davis had not expected to hear from Kerry, and Kerry would have been just as happy to not see another government agent as long as she lived. But they came into her life for a reason, and she figured she'd use it to her advantage.

The agent was waiting on a bench next to the water beside the museum. Kerry had asked her to meet there after Wayne's funeral.

The funeral along with finding out that Amy was responsible for Katie's death had made it an emotional day for everyone. Simon and Josh took the boat out onto the lake to spend some time together, while Oliver and Thomas took the kids to Lisa's café for a treat.

As Kerry walked toward the waterfront, she realized how much of the small town reminded her of Wayne. There wasn't a street, shop, or holiday that would be free of his memory. And although she knew it would make her sad, it would also ensure that he'd always be alive everywhere she went.

Serena Davis slid to the side and made room as Raven jumped onto the bench. He began to sniff, then lick Serena, and Kerry realized she could have used Raven to figure out that Serena and Ronan were not the danger she needed to be worried about.

"How did today go?" Serena asked as she rubbed the back of Raven's ear.

"Sad, but it was important to do," Kerry's words stuck in her throat and she began to cry. It was too soon to talk about Wayne, at least not without crying.

"The microchip you gave us had all the information we needed," Serena said. "Ronan is bringing it to the President now."

John Doe's real name was Tim Bates. Kerry had learned when she stumbled into the secret room on Airplane Island, that he was working with Ronan and Serena in a joint operation between the U.S. and Canada. At the height of the pandemic, various groups opposed to foreign intervention with the vaccines were trying to sabotage the production facilities. Initial intelligence had pointed to independent representatives in the American government that were secretly funding the attacks. Tim approached Ronan and offered his help to collect information to prove what Dennis Nathanson had been doing. As a U.S. Senator, Nathanson had evaded suspicion concerning any illegal involvement in the attacks.

Knowing that it was possibly someone within the executive branch of the government, their operation had to remain secretive. Once inside, Tim also established that it involved a group in Canada as well.

"Tim had managed to download some information from his final meeting with Nathanson, but he died before he could hand it over. When he downloaded the information onto a backup system, it automatically scanned into the microchip. The information we needed to prove who was involved in both countries was stored on the microchip. His computer was set up to transmit the information automatically from his backup system to the microchip," Serena explained. "We were able to patch into the security film at the restaurant you narrowed down with the food you found in his system. And that's when we saw he was meeting with Dennis Nathanson."

"But why here? Why Lake Pines?" Kerry asked.

"The man who formed our secret operation owns that cabin. It's a place he likes to fly up to and do some fishing. Off the grid, of course."

"Of course."

They sat quietly, contemplating their conversation and everything that had happened over the last few days.

"And the group responsible for poisoning Tim Bates?" Kerry asked.

Serena smiled, "Ronan's taking them into custody today."

"I've been curious about something," Kerry asked.

Serena nodded, "About?"

"The myth about Airplane Island. Is it true?"

Serena smiled, "Yes, but it's not about what happened that unique, but about who was flying the plane when it crashed."

Kerry listened as Serena mentioned a name she hadn't heard in years, mostly because everyone had believed this man had been shot twelve years earlier. She was sworn to secrecy, however, even if she wasn't Kerry didn't think she'd want to be heard repeating a story that most would label as a conspiracy theory. So she agreed to stay silent.

The revelation about Tim Bates and the group that was trying to stop vaccine production in North America was something that Kerry found far more frightening. Although they both knew it wasn't something that would be reported in the papers, they understood that some justice was found, and in the end, Kerry was glad she was able to be a part of making that happen. As the setting sun warmed their faces, they sat quietly next to each other on the small park bench and hoped that there would be fewer victims and more survivors in the coming days.

45

A sharp August wind surrounded Carly, yet she refused to turn away, facing the biting sting of the gust head-on. She hadn't returned to the property, where a decade earlier the painful part of her past was buried. Both figuratively and literally.

She had never wanted to, nor had she needed to, but today was different.

It had been a while, and even if Josh hadn't called her and requested she meet him here, it would have been time.

Did Josh know? Was it time to face what they had done?

Just a few days earlier at Wayne's funeral, and sitting a few rows behind Josh and Simon, Carly found it impossible to lift her face to either of them. The tears she shed were not just tears for a lost friend, but they were tears that fell for the man who rescued her from what would have been a certain jail sentence.

At the time, it wouldn't have been seen as a young girl pulling away from an attack, but a girl pushing one of the town's favored athletes and students to his death. It wasn't fair, but it was the way things would have been viewed at that time.

Carly knew that, and so did Wayne.

She listened to the eulogies at Wayne's funeral reveal the stories of the hundreds of young girls and boys that he saved during his time working in the National Human Trafficking Task Force. Across the country, families and survivors recognized their freedom and future were owed to Wayne's actions. There were points during that day that she wanted to reveal what he had done for her, but she knew she couldn't. Outside of her father, they were the only ones aware of what happened. She thought no one else knew.

That was until Danny Blythe had approached her. Simon revealed to Carly that Benji was the associate Danny referred to and, after he explained the events of the night on the pier, they both fell silent. They never spoke of Benji's death or the part Simon had in shooting him. They both seemed to know that it was better if they didn't speak of it.

The deaths of Danny Blythe and Benji Jones had finally freed her from the threat hanging over her head, and she wondered when it would start to make her feel better. Or if Josh's call meant revealing the past that she fought to keep buried.

These were the thoughts that rolled through Carly's mind as she stood next to the hill that rolled away from the cabin, into the woods - and where John Turshen lay buried.

The grass had filled in the rectangular plot where an unmarked grave had been dug in haste. The night had been darker than most in August of that year, and it was cool and dry. The idea was her father's but the location was Wayne's contribution.

The first drops of rain began to fall as they stomped the ground flat after filling in the hole. A small mound remained and Wayne assured her that it would flatten over time and soon the grass would regrow in that patch, leaving no trace of what they had done. The rain continued for a full week and the gray, cold days that stretched into colder evenings, mirrored Carly's emotions. Eventually, she was able to put the memory of what happened behind her, but she never really forgot.

Nothing could erase the memory of that night or what they had done. Carly's eyes went directly to the area on the hill where John Turshen lay. The ground was the same level as the surrounding area on the hill and the grass had returned, filling in the gap just as Wayne had promised. To anyone else looking out over the hill on the property, it was just that. A hill.

The cabin had fallen into a dilapidated state. Where glass window panes had once kept out rain and birds, gaping holes now offered an easy entrance. Although the frame was straight and the roof intact, the paint had faded from the siding and a few stones had been knocked loose from the chimney. The front steps remained in place and Carly stepped up and onto the landing, pausing where the front door used to hang. A wind blew unobstructed through the cabin, sweeping the memories of Christmases and holidays away. Piles of leaves accumulated in the corner and a musty scent, left by the rodents that had taken over the once-loved family retreat, filled the air.

The room felt small and cold. Yet, the cabin remained, resolutely attached to the land.

She was vaguely aware of the slamming car door, and the approaching steps up the hollow porch. Carly turned around at the sound of his voice, commanding but filled with concern, as he said her name.

Josh was as tall as Wayne, a family trait that both of their parents were blessed with and something neither of her boys would inherit from her or Kenny. But unlike Wayne, Josh was trim. Lithe and muscular with a runner's body, while Wayne had the build of a defensive tackle. His midnight-black hair was cut short and brushed to the side, and while Wayne always seemed to struggle with a style, it always came easily to Josh. However, the one thing that the two brothers had in common was the calm emotion that filled their eyes.

Although he saw the upset in Carly's face, he didn't understand the extent of the sadness that she had buried.

"Thanks for meeting me out here," Josh's words echoed inside the empty cabin and his eyes drifted around the space. "It's hard to believe that this place seemed so big to me at one time. Now it's just a run-down shed."

Carly looked around and nodded. Unable to see anything but Wayne standing at the window waiting as she and her father arrived on that rain-filled night a decade ago.

"I'm just not sure why you wanted me to come here," Carly said. Her words and tone measured, not revealing the anxiousness that rested at the base of her throat.

"It's about Wayne."

Carly gasped and held in that breath as she waited for Josh to continue. Her cheeks grew warm and her blood pulsed, echoing through her ears.

Josh reached into his pocket and pulled out a white envelope and handed it to Carly. Her hand shook as she reached toward Josh's hand and slipped the envelope from his grasp.

"He wanted me to give this to you," Josh said, motioning to the envelope, and then to the space around them.

"I don't get it?" Carly's voice was shaky and her words formed as a question.

She hesitated to open the envelope, aware of the only thing it could contain was the secret that they carried between them for the last ten years.

"Wayne wanted you to have this property," Josh explained. "I was with his lawyer earlier today, and Wayne was very clear in his Will that this property in its entirety be left to you."

"But, it's your family place. You should have it."

Josh shook his head, "It was never as important to me as it was to Wayne, and if he wanted you to have it he must've had a really good reason."

Josh's eyes watched Carly with more curiosity than leeriness. Josh had known Carly his whole life, and it never occurred to him that Wayne and she had a relationship. Not that it would have mattered, it was just odd he never mentioned it.

Josh reached out and rested his warm hand on Carly's shoulder, and she stopped shaking almost immediately, "Maybe someday you'll feel like you can explain why you and Wayne were so close. Until then, accept his gift. There was a reason he wanted you to have it, and you have my complete blessing."

Carly wrinkled her face and turned away. She didn't want Josh to see the flood of tears she could no longer hold back. His hand slipped from her shoulder but she could feel him move closer until he wrapped his arms around her body.

They cried together, like two old friends mourning the loss of a man that was important in both of their lives, and unsure of how they would move forward. The changing light in the sky, dimmed over the property, stretching the shadows of the trees and their bodies, and a murder of crows cawed and circled above the roof's peak.

Season changes came with a sense of betrayal. The loss of light, warmth, and long days would soon be gone, replaced with the deep freeze of several months. However, this year, winter would be filled with healing as everyone tried to come to terms with the loss of Wayne in their lives.

Carly followed Josh out of the cabin and watched from the front step as he drove away. Before she realized what she was doing, she walked toward the hill that stretched out behind the cabin and stood next to the spot where John Turshen was buried.

As if by invitation, glowing fireflies filled the night air, infusing the stark black night with streaks of light. Wavering and circling in the space around her. A gust of wind picked up force and rolled over the hill. The fireflies began to leave, one by one as they lost their fight with the wind until all that remained was the night sky and Carly standing next to the grave where John Turshen lay.

She returned to her car, walking the uneven path with her head held high. She would create something special with the gift Wayne left her, something that would honor his sacrifice all those years ago.

But before she could do that, Carly had to free herself from the secret that filled her life.

Kenny would be waiting at home with their two boys, confused by the events of the last week. He had never pushed to know the reason why Carly had been at Danny Blythe's cabin or questioned why she had spent days in a deep depression when she heard about Wayne's death. And when Carly cried long into the night following Wayne's funeral, Kenny just held her until she was calm.

Tonight, however, Carly would release her secret and trust that Kenny would not only understand but would help keep it buried. And then she could be free, at least as much as she could manage to be.

46

The file on Wayne's autopsy and examination sat in the middle of Kerry's desk. Filing it away would mean that all doors were closed on Wayne, or at least it would feel that way. Kerry still couldn't believe he was gone and she'd find herself doubled over and crying when she would think of him.

It was a physical pain she would feel like a knot in her gut. Anger would be the only emotion that would pull her away from her sadness. She wanted Alex to pay with his life but knew she'd have to settle with his life behind bars. Kerry knew that Alex wasn't worth the time she devoted to thinking about him, but Wayne was worth it.

She owed him her life on so many levels. And she couldn't imagine going forward without him. The photos of Wayne in frames at home, his contact information in her phone, and now the file that sat on her desk. Kerry couldn't get rid of any reminder of Wayne. She pulled open the desk drawer and slid the file inside.

When she was ready, she'd deal with the file, but not before that moment.

Josh and Thomas were stopping by for dinner and they were going to plan a private memorial together. Wayne was family, and that meant Josh was too. She turned the lights off, locked the door, and walked to her car.

Her breath floated in front of her face, a small puffy cloud dispersed just as quickly as it appeared and Kerry sighed. This year winter would come early, and they would be in a deep freeze and bound up tight in their homes for months.

This time it wouldn't be the pandemic that kept them housebound, but the unrelenting frost in the air and the ice on the ground. Whether it was the climate or government restrictions, staying inside for long periods felt like a prison sentence and not the cozy retreat they had felt before. This year she and Simon vowed to make every day count for Dominique. And with Wayne gone too soon and so violently, she knew they'd be committed to keeping their promise.

Her car's engine purred to life and the heater blew a soft warmth over her hands as she gripped the steering wheel. The corner of a small white envelope caught her eye as it fluttered in front of the vent. It was laying in the center of the console, tucked into the cup holder next to her seat. The light script was distinct and she recognized it as Agent Miller's. There could only be one thing in the envelope that was of any interest to Kerry.

Information about Dominique's birth parents was the driving force that convinced Kerry to work with Agent Miller in the first place. Waynes death kept her from pursuing the answer any further. She had decided that if she was going to find out, it wasn't going to be at the expense of people she loved, and she had forgotten all about Agent Miller's promise. Kerry pulled the envelope out of the cup holder and slipped her finger in the small opening at the back. There was a small rip and then Kerry stopped. She pulled her finger from the paper and lowered it to her lap.

The knowledge of who Dominique's birth father was could bring the exact problems her father had warned her about. Kerry had a pretty good idea of who the father was, and she shuddered at the thought of that man being anywhere near her daughter. Kerry folded the envelope in half and tucked it deep in her pocket. Neither Simon nor her father would know that she received this, and she wasn't even sure she was going to keep it. What she was sure of was that she'd protect Dominique with her life, and if that meant keeping her away from her birth father, then that's what she'd do.

And against her best intentions, Kerry would keep this one last secret from Simon.

47

Josh was packing the last few items of Wayne's into a box that Sally gave him when Simon knocked on the door.

"Wayne never really left Lake Pines, did he?" Josh asked but didn't really expect an answer. "There's stuff in these drawers from his first day."

Josh held up a collection of photographs and notices that Wayne had saved from his first few years working for the department.

"Here's one of you," Josh laughed and handed it to Simon.

"That was on the day I wrote my first ticket," Simon smiled. "Wayne teased me that it would be uphill from there."

Simon handed it back to Josh and then changed his mind and slipped it into his pocket.

"What are your plans now?" Simon asked as Josh closed the lid on the small box.

Josh rested his forearms on the box and looked around the office, "I guess the house is next."

"Have you considered keeping it?"

Josh shook his head, "Wayne was living here and it made sense for him to keep it after our parents died."

Simon stepped into the office and closed the door.

"I just got off the phone with Peter," Simon sat down in a chair that was pushed against the wall. "Lukas has requested a position on the Human Trafficking Task Force."

Josh's eyes widened, "Really? I didn't see that coming."

"Neither did I, to tell you the truth."

"What do you think about that?"

Simon shrugged his shoulders, "Lukas is a bright kid, and he's been impressive the few years I've worked with him. I saw firsthand during the pandemic that not much fazed him. He knows how to stay calm and cool in some pretty tense situations."

"He was also quite affected by what we found in the shipping container on the pier."

Simon agreed, "He said that working with Wayne really opened his eyes to what was happening to so many young vulnerable kids in the country and he wanted to make a difference."

"That's why we all got into this crazy profession, I guess," Josh understood Lukas' desire to get involved, it's what drew Wayne into the task force. "I hope he can make a difference."

"So do I," Simon agreed. "However, that leaves me short an officer. And with George Crompt retiring in a month we're going to need to do some recruiting."

Simon raised his brows and tilted his head, "So what do you think?"

"Me?" Josh stabbed his thumb in the center of his chest. "Here?"

"Why not?" Simon countered. "I know you and Thomas have talked about simplifying your lives, and moving to a smaller town could do that."

Josh nodded, it was obviously something he and Thomas had talked about and it wasn't the first time he had considered a move from Toronto to Lake Pines. Simon could see it in his friend's eyes.

"And then there's the treehouse," Simon smiled.

"Yes, there's that," a wide grin stretched across Josh's face at the memory of spending so much of his youth suspended in the play structure that doubled as a sanctuary.

As Josh thought about the prospect of the move and working in Lake Pines, his smile softened and the corner of his eyes curled as the idea took hold.

"Let me talk to Thomas," Josh lifted the box and tucked it under his arm. "I'll let you know what we decide."

Simon opened the door and before Josh left he wrapped his arms around him. He embraced his best friend's little brother, who was also his friend since childhood, and he knew somewhere deep inside that the move is what Wayne would've wanted.

And as Josh smiled and turned to leave, he felt it too.

48

Dominique stirred in her crib as Kerry slipped into her room. A sliver of moonlight inched across the floor and spilled over the back of the rocking horse. The horse was tucked in the corner waiting for the day that Dominique could ride it. Kerry's eyes filled with tears as she thought of Wayne and the hours he spent cutting and then sanding pieces of pinewood until he perfected the shape and finish of the horse. The silky wool he braided into a mane and tail hung motionless until the moment that Dominique would weave her fingers through each strand and hold on tight.

Wayne wouldn't hear his goddaughter squeal with delight as she rocked the horse for the first time and he would miss the tight embrace of Dominique's arms around his neck. But he would still be with her, Kerry felt it down deep inside. He had to be. It was the only way she could remember him without crying.

Kerry looked over the side of Dominique's crib and she remembered the words Wayne said to her the day before he died.

He tried to convince her to focus on Dominique and not place her energy where information could bring her pain. He didn't want her to bring something dark and foreboding into their lives. Kerry felt like he knew something and was holding back information he believed would hurt her, but she never had the chance to ask him. Only now did Kerry realize that Wayne had uncovered who Katie Lancaster really was.

Raven pushed his nose against Kerry's leg, and she reached down and stroked his head. His tail wagged and his eyes drifted toward the sleeping baby.

Kerry reached down and lifted Dominique and cradled her in her arm, and then lowered herself into the chair in the corner. She buried her nose into the soft, messy curls that edged her daughter's face, and breathed in. Kerry had been consumed with searching for the information she believed Dominique needed, but had forgotten that all her daughter wanted was this. The late-night snuggles and morning routine, and the feeling of security and love. All of which she already had.

The envelope had been tucked in the back of her drawer, resealed and hidden until Kerry decided what she was going to do with it. The answers she was looking for, the ones she once believed Dominique needed, were contained in those pieces of paper. Kerry eventually read the pages, unable to ignore the envelope any longer. The knowledge of who Dominique's birth parents were, did not come with the peaceful knowledge she hoped it would. Instead the knowledge of who Katie's parents were somehow frightened her more than the fact that Alex Johnson was Dominique's birth father. Katie was her real name, Lancaster was her grandmother's maiden name. She wanted to remain removed from the knowledge of who her parents were. The information was much more easily obtained with Agent Miller's access and came because the government had been monitoring the human trafficking operation and had intimate knowledge of who Alex was, which also included the people close to him. A simple DNA test confirmed that he was the father, and a copy was included in the letter Agent Miller left in her car.

Each time Kerry thought about why she wanted to know, she questioned whether it really was for Dominique or for her.

Insecurity at not being Dominique's birth mom was a feeling she was warned about experiencing, something she read about on a parenting blog and it was sneaking into her relationship with her daughter. She convinced herself that she didn't want to wait for Dominique to reach the inconsolable teenage years where her rebellion against her parents was expressed in a search for her 'real mom'.

No. Kerry was going to be prepared. She'd have all the information in advance and know who should be contacted, where they'd be, and then she'd avoid the guilty shouts and accusations.

Dominique squirmed and readjusted her head in the space between Kerry's shoulder and neck and then fell back into a cooing slumber. Her soft lips pressed against Kerry's neck and brought an overwhelming surge of love that washed over her.

The pandemic showed her that life was unpredictable, and for the most part, everyone was unprepared. When restrictions were put in place and rules were imposed, there was confusion and anger. Accusations of rights that had been violated as Kerry pulled another sheet over another victim taken so unfairly by the invisible weapon.

How, Kerry wondered, would she explain the first year of Dominique's life to her?

The world they lived in, that Dominique was born into, had turned dystopian almost overnight. And almost as seamlessly, things returned to normal.

The outbreak was silenced by the vaccine but was the lesson to humanity forgotten? Memories weren't so easy for anyone working on the frontlines to push down.

While the shelter-in-place order was imposed on most of the global population, Kerry and Simon were thrust into the midst of a fight. While online forums for homemade sourdough bread, and handmade masks flourished and produced endless memes, Kerry was pronouncing another life lost to the virus.

Once the vaccines began to take hold, and the battle lines were shifting in their favor, people emerged changed. Those who were more resilient to life and eager to make changes quit their jobs and ended relationships. Vowing to not live whatever time they had left in unfulfilling arrangements. Some close friends who previously embraced each other without thought now feared the slightest contact.

Kisses and handshakes became symbols of invasion and a smile to a stranger on the street seemed unnatural.

Then there were those that embraced everything and everyone around them more gently. People they loved, they pulled closer. Differing opinions were met with more understanding and patience.

That which we cannot control...was released.

Those were the bearers of hope.

She knew she couldn't protect and shelter Dominique from every painful inevitability in her life, and that all she could do was prepare her to be strong when the time called for it. Kerry would leave the envelope sealed until the day Dominique would be ready. In the end, Kerry could tell Dominique that they found justice for Katie Lancaster and that she loved her from the moment she was conceived.

A breeze blew through the small crack in the window and brushed across the floor. Dominique stirred, and Kerry pulled her close, and as the rocking horse stirred in the corner, Kerry smiled.

Everything would finally be alright, after all.

The End

Thank you for reading, and I sincerely hope you enjoyed the seventh book in the Lake Pines Mystery Series, ***Deadly Past.***

If you enjoyed ***Deadly Past***, I would sincerely appreciate it if you would take a moment and leave a review.

Thanks, and have a wonderful day.

L.L. Abbott

Books by L.L. Abbott

Mystery & Suspense

Thrillers

Teen & Young Adult

General Fiction/Rom Com

Made in the USA
Monee, IL
31 October 2022